THE PRICE OF HAPPINESS

After her father's death, Charlotte Hargreaves discovers that she must sell the family farm, Deepdale Manor, to pay the death duties. James Thornton has a good eye for business and can see the benefits of buying the farm for the land it stands on. When he arrives to view the property, Charlie sees him as the enemy. Yet she finds herself attracted to him, and it takes all her strength to remain free to oppose his plans.

Books by Louise Armstrong
in the Linford Romance Library:

HOLD ON TO PARADISE
JAPANESE MAGIC
A PICTURE OF HAPPINESS

LOUISE ARMSTRONG

THE PRICE OF HAPPINESS

Complete and Unabridged

LINFORD
Leicester

First published in Great Britain in 2000

First Linford Edition
published 2001

British Library CIP Data

Armstrong, Louise
    The price of happiness.—Large print ed.—
    Linford romance library
    1. Love stories
    2. Large type books
    I. Title
    823.9'14 [F]

    ISBN 0–7089–9723–6

Published by
F. A. Thorpe (Publishing)
Anstey, Leicestershire

Set by Words & Graphics Ltd.
Anstey, Leicestershire
Printed and bound in Great Britain by
T. J. International Ltd., Padstow, Cornwall

This book is printed on acid-free paper

1

'Don't forget that property fellow from London is coming to look around the estate this morning, Charlotte,' the burly farmhand said.

A slim girl in a red-checked shirt looked up and shook her head at him. Her eyes had violet smudges under them, reflecting the sleepless nights she'd suffered since her father died.

'I haven't forgotten,' she said briefly, and turned back to her task of pouring petrol into the power saw that sat on the grass in front of her.

'Are you not going to show him round?' the farmhand persisted, looking at her mournfully.

The smell of petrol was making Charlotte, Charlie to her friends, feel sick, and the metal teeth of the saw suddenly reminded her of a huge, hungry shark, like the one approaching her family farm at this very minute.

'I've left Harry Pickles to show him around,' she said.

'Harry? He won't be any good as a salesman.'

'Exactly,' she replied tensely.

The big farmhand gave her another doleful look.

'Stop looking at me as if I was machine-gunning kittens!' Charlotte exploded. 'Do you want this money merchant to buy Deepdale? Modernise it? Change everything?'

'Nay, Charlotte, lass, of course I don't. It's just that your father would never have treated a guest so badly.'

'This man is not a guest,' Charlotte said grimly. 'He's the enemy. Let's not forget that.'

The enemy, otherwise known as James Thornton, was standing on the gravel in front of Deepdale Manor, and he was temporarily at a loss. A little mole of a man stood in the sunshine grinning at James. Faded blue eyes peeped out beneath the brim of a woolly hat. He had a jumper that was mostly holes, breeches tied up in a mad tangle of string, and displayed a wide grin. James didn't want to hurt the old countryman's feelings, but he was a man on a mission.

'How many acres did you say?' he asked again.

'Thump!' Harry Pickles said. 'Frump, thump.'

To give himself time to think, James turned away from the old man, took off his pearl-grey jacket, folded it carefully and placed it on the seat of the Range Rover he'd hired for this trip to the country. The May sunshine was bright on the new paintwork. He saw his sunglasses lying on the dashboard. They would cut out the glare. He put them on and turned back to his problem guide.

Now that he could see more clearly, he noticed the old man's hat wasn't really a hat but a knitted tea-cosy! Next he noticed that the blue eyes under the tea-cosy were peeping at him with the sharp expression he associated with the negotiating table.

'You've been playing me for a fool,' James said slowly.

The old man smiled innocently and tried to wave James down a gravel path that led down the side of the house. James smiled just as innocently.

'I want you to take me to the farm manager, please.'

The old man met James's eyes for a long, measuring second, then he heaved a defeated sigh.

'Yump,' he said sadly.

The tea-cosy nodded in submission. He slowly and reluctantly showed James a different path entirely.

'Is the farm manager up there?' James asked, following the old man. 'Charlie Hargreaves, isn't it? Have I got the chap's name right?'

Harry screeched to a halt and shook his head violently.

'Nump!'

'Never mind,' James said, holding up one hand in warning. 'We'll sort all that out when I get there. Just lead the way.'

'Gump,' Harry said, and this time he trotted up the path that led to the fields where Charlie was working.

Not knowing that her plan to outwit the London visitor had been blown away like a snowflake in an oven, Charlie was intent on the mint-green pine tree she was about to cut down. She had already calculated where she wanted it to fall, and tied a rope high up around the pink bark of the trunk.

'You'll have to keep the rope taut,' she warned the farmhand standing next to her. 'Stand well back, and be ready to pull hard when the tree starts to topple.'

'Yes, Charlie,' he said. 'Shall I take the dog with me? He hates the noise of the saw.'

'Good idea,' Charlie said, nodding. She clicked her fingers at her little white Jack Russell terrier.

'Bingo, go with Sam.'

She watched them walk down the

narrow track that separated the green-houses from the old stables. Then she looked back at the tree, squinting against the sun. The old Scots pine had been so badly storm-damaged that it was in severe danger of landing on the greenhouses. She hated to cut down a tree, but if she didn't fell it in a controlled manner, it could do a lot of damage.

The farmhand waved to show he was ready. Charlie put on her padded ear-mufflers and pulled the starting cord. The saw kicked noisily into life. She picked it up, waved it in a determined manner and took a deep breath as she marched over to the thick, upwardly thrusting trunk of the pine tree. As usual, she fully expected to win her battle with the forces of nature.

Meanwhile, as he walked through the greenhouses, James's sharp eyes noticed the sad lack of paint and many missing panes of glass. Good, he thought, that will bring the price down nicely! The metallic roar of the power saw grew louder, but James carried on walking. He was startled when a hand gripped his arm and dragged him back.

'Gump!' Harry warned.

'What?' James asked.

Then he heard a deep, slow, creaking sound, and for an insane moment he thought that a giant was throwing a toothbrush at him. Then he recognised branches, not bristles, and realised that it was a tree falling slowly and heavily along the middle of the track he had been walking along.

'Oh, thanks.'

The ground juddered as the tree bounced three times before settling. Clouds of dust flew up as its branches splintered, and aromatic pine resin filled the air. It lay tidily in the direct centre of the path. Not one of its branches had touched a building.

'Nice work,' James murmured.

He admired efficiency wherever he found it. Perhaps this farm manager, Charles Hargreaves, would be easy to do business with. James might have had an inside tip about grants from the European parliament, but he had no idea how to go about flattening a messy old farm like this one and turning it into an agri-business. Maybe the farm manager was the man to help him.

It was a profit-making opportunity not to be missed. James had hunted carefully for a farm that would qualify for the maximum grant, and he knew that as soon as the new scheme became public, Deepdale Manor would double or even triple in value.

The figure before him straightened up and pulled off the ear-protectors. James decided he'd better keep his secret for a while longer, because the farm manager was now taking off a hard safety helmet, and in the process revealing a long, feminine blonde plait.

'You felled that tree perfectly,' he called, admiring her whipcord strength as he approached.

She looked at him with clear, freezing eyes.

'What can I do for you?' she asked,

ignoring his previous remark and brushing at the snowfall of sawdust that drifted all over her clothes.

James couldn't stop his eyes following the path of her delicate hands as they brushed over her slender body. She was curved in all the right places, but what was she wearing? Oil-stained jeans, army boots and a ripped check shirt! James liked groomed and glossy women who wore beautiful clothes. He looked calmly into the scornful grey eyes, stretched out his hand and gave her his best smile.

'Good morning.'

She ignored his hand and glared at him, planting her hands on her hips. Fine dark brows arched over the challenging expression in her eyes and the lashes were the longest he'd ever seen. Glossy strands of fair hair escaped her plait and curled softly around her heart-shaped face, but James was just beginning to realise that there was nothing else soft about this woman. As they stared at each other, a small white Jack Russell terrier came running over to see what was going on.

'Hello, fella,' James said, glad of the diversion and, looking directly into Charlie's eyes, he asked her, 'or is he a she?'

'He,' she answered reluctantly, shifting her eyes away from his. 'And Bingo hates strangers. He'll bite you.'

As if on cue, the dog wrinkled its brown nose and growled warningly.

'You won't bite me, will you, Bingo?'

James made his voice low and soothing and held out a hand. The dog gave a cautious sniff.

'I warned you,' Charlie snapped.

'He won't bite me,' James said.

At the sound of his deep male voice, the hairs along the back of the dog's spine went down. James looked at the terrier again.

'Bingo's a good dog, aren't you?' he said soothingly.

The little dog capitulated completely. Wagging its ridiculous stump of a tail, it ran over and begged James to scratch its tummy.

'Traitor!' Charlie said bitterly to her dog.

James straightened up and looked at her with a smile in his eyes.

'Dogs are said to be good judges of character,' he pronounced teasingly. 'On Bingo's recommendation, won't you trust me?'

Trust you, Charlie thought! I'd sooner trust a shark in a goldfish pond! She wasn't fooled by the film-star good looks of the man who stood laughing in the sunshine. He might have dimples and eyes the exact blue of the sky above, but she could see the primitive male strength that lay below his city clothes. He was a shark, all right, and she was very afraid that she was on his menu.

To escape his mocking glare, she looked down and brushed at the sawdust on her clothes. It might have worked as a delaying tactic, but it exposed the fact that her hands were shaking. Charlie swallowed. Her throat was dry. Why had he shattered her composure so quickly?

Obviously realising that she had no intention of shaking it, he had dropped his hand. A slight tightness around his lips was the only indication he gave that he'd noticed her rudeness.

'Can you tell me where I'll find the farm manager?' he asked coolly.

His deep, velvety voice made the hair prickle on the back of Charlie's neck. She could hear power, decision and the hint of a threat there.

'I'm the farm manager,' she snapped.

'Really?'

One lazy black eyebrow went up in amusement. His deep blue eyes were twin gleams of mockery.

'I wouldn't have guessed that.'

'What's the matter?' Charlie asked sweetly.

Somehow she had to fight this man.

'Are you surprised that a woman can run a farm as big as this one?'

Amusement twisted his wide mouth.

'I'm surprised that the farm manager is making such a poor job of showing around a prospective buyer.'

Charlie went hot and cold as she wrestled with her feelings. He'd be right in his assessment, if this were just a job to her. But her whole life was at stake. She felt like a very small minnow threatened by a very large shark, but she wouldn't give in.

'Harry knows the farm as well as I do,' she countered defiantly.

James shook his head slightly. Her whole body prickled in reaction as she met the awareness in his eyes. She battled to hold on to her rapidly dissolving authority.

'I'm too busy to show you around myself,' she muttered.

His gaze was ironic and his tone dripped with sarcasm.

'I didn't ask you, personally, to do it,' he pointed out.

Charlie's self-esteem crumbled under his unshakeable self-confidence.

'Sam — '

She broke off in horror and put her hands to her throat. Her voice sounded like a mouse squeak. She cleared her throat and pointed at the farmhand.

'Sam will take you,' she said gruffly.

James gave her an unexpectedly attractive smile but then he turned away as if she were of no further interest.

'Lead the way, Sam,' he said.

He set off through the sparkling green grass of the meadow with a long stride that made Charlie think of a panther. Sam lumbered along behind him, looking more like a hippo in rubber boots.

Forcing down her vivid imagination, Charlie tried to collect herself. She felt as if he'd won a small victory, but she'd be ready for him next time.

'And as for you,' she said to her little dog, 'how could you be such a creep, Bingo?'

Bingo lay down and put his nose on his paws. Charlie softened and threw him one of the dog treats she kept in her pocket, and the stump of his tail thumped to show she was forgiven. She picked up an axe and started trimming side limbs off the tree she had just felled. Wordlessly, old Harry picked up another axe and started hacking branches off the other side.

'He out-manoeuvred us there! We'll have to think of a battle plan, Harry,' Charlie said.

The old man didn't answer. He kept his head down and continued to chop steadily at the branches.

'Well, I'll think of a plan then,' Charlie muttered, but it was hard to think of war on such a glorious day.

Lark song poured down from the blue vault of the sky, and the summer smell of crushed grass was strong. Charlie leaned on the pine-scented trunk of the tree for a moment and closed her eyes in the warm sunshine, listening to the birds. The song clearest in spring, when the males sought out the females, and nature bonded them tight to create a family unit.

Charlie shook herself angrily. She despised domesticity in all its forms. Farming was what interested her, and a good morning's work was the best way to get back to normal. But as Charlie got on with her woodcutting, she was aware of a strange sensation prickling over her sensitive skin. It made it difficult to concentrate.

Finally Charlie decided that sawdust must have got into her underclothes. She would have to go back to the house at lunchtime and get changed.

2

As Charlie approached the house at lunchtime, she saw the car that belonged to her neighbour and unofficial fiancé, Quentin Rafferty, was parked on the gravel sweep next to James's Range Rover.

Charlie kicked off her boots at the kitchen door and padded down the cool stone flags of the hall in her thickly-socked feet. Bingo's claws clicked as he followed behind her. Sunlight fell in bars through the leaded glass windows. It was all so familiar, the smell of lilac and furniture polish, and a radio playing upstairs, but Charlie knew the air of sanctuary was an illusion. Anything could happen now this money man was here.

Quentin was sitting at the kitchen table, his old anorak on the chair behind him.

'Hello, darling,' he said.

Charlie saw that he was still sporting his ragged, ginger beard. Her hints about shaving just weren't getting through. She let him kiss her cheek to make up for her unkind thoughts about him.

'What have you done with that pansy from the city?' Quentin asked.

Misery swept over Charlie.

'He's a shark, not a pansy!' she told Quentin. 'I'm afraid he'll buy us out. He's the kind of man who goes all out for what he wants, and gets it.'

She took a step towards Quentin. She needed comforting. He hated displays of emotion and stepped back sharply to avoid her. There was a sharp yap. Quentin clutched his ankle, then he kicked out at the dog. Bingo scuttled into the dog basket. His little head popped up and he seemed to be laughing at Quentin out of one naughty brown eye.

'That damned dog!' Quentin swore.

'I'll have none of that language in my

kitchen,' Charlie's housekeeper said. 'What did you go standing on the dog for, if you didn't want biting?'

Martha Bird bustled over to the oak dresser and took some blue-patterned plates off the shelves.

'Well, Master Quentin, I see you arrived just in time for lunch, again.'

'It's the smell of your deliciously lovely cooking that attracts me,' Quentin said, trying to humour her.

'That's how flies find the muck heap,' Martha muttered.

Charlie didn't try to reprimand her. For some reason the old Yorkshire woman disliked Quentin, and Martha had been grimly satisfied when Quentin's visits had fallen off after Charlie's father died.

'You'll not see him again now he knows there's no money,' Martha had said, and Charlie had begun to believe her, but here was Quentin, sitting in the kitchen again, just like old times.

Martha went to the oven and took out a huge shepherd's pie. She dished out two portions.

'Eat up,' she said, putting them on the table. 'I'll eat with the men later.'

'Have a cup of tea with us, Martha,' Charlie said.

Martha nodded and went to fetch the teapot. Quentin raised an eyebrow.

'Eating with the help?' he hissed.

Charlie felt really angry.

'Martha keeps this place going!' she whispered, and as Martha came back to the table she added in a louder voice, 'I wish we could pay Jane to come more often, Martha. You've been cleaning since six o'clock.'

The housekeeper sat at the table and poured a cup of tea.

'The bed and breakfast doesn't make enough to warrant extra help,' she said sadly. 'We've only one room booked for tonight.'

'I think you should spend more money on advertising,' Quentin said.

'I would if I could afford it,' Charlie said.

'Talking of brass,' Martha added,

'have you raised enough to buy Deepdale?'

'I'm talking to people I know,' Quentin muttered, 'but I need more time.'

'Time is what we don't have,' Charlie said, thinking of James steamrollering over her that morning. 'He moves fast.'

Martha took a sip of her tea.

'Happen you can persuade him to make a fast decision against buying Deepdale.'

'Put him off?' Quentin asked.

'Invent a ghost,' Martha added. 'Tell him the well is poisoned, anything to frighten him away.'

Quentin slapped the table with his hand.

'Got it! Lure him into Destiny Caves, and then accidentally lose him. He's a city guy so he'll hate it!'

'I don't know, Quentin,' Charlie said. 'It's a mean thing to do, and I'd never forgive myself if he got hurt.'

'The only danger is flooding,' Quentin said, 'and this has been the driest

May in recorded history. I'll check the weather report.'

He picked up the local newspaper, and his eyebrows shot up briefly. Then a small smile played about his lips as he read out loud, 'Outlook, fine and dry.'

He folded the newspaper and put it in his pocket and Charlie looked at the older woman for some guidance.

'I don't know. Martha, what do you think I should do?'

'Think about what will happen to us all if this London man buys Deepdale and turns us all out. What will happen to Harry Pickles? To you? What if Sam Hartley has to give up the farm cottage, his wife with a new baby and all?'

'You think I should do it?'

'I think you should fight back somehow.'

'Then I'll do it!' Charlie declared.

The door into the kitchen banged open and in walked James, followed by Sam, the farmhand. Charlie felt the way she did before a storm. The air was charged with tension. She felt guilty, and her heart began to race. James dropped into the seat at the head of the table as if he were born to it.

'Your man gave me a good tour, thank you, Charlie. Too bad the dry weather has adversely affected the silage this year.'

'What do you know about silage?' Charlie snapped.

'Only what Sam told me,' James retorted, 'and a poor harvest affects the price of farmland.'

Sam, who had been looking pleased at the compliment, realised that James had outwitted him, and looked guiltily at his feet. Martha looked as if she'd like to give Sam a rare scolding, but she pressed her lips together and contented herself with banging the lunch plates on to the table.

'Thank you,' James said, smiling at her before picking up his knife and fork. 'This looks special.'

'Of course, the bed and breakfast business is very strong,' Quentin said, and Charlie blessed him for his support. 'I can't see a man like you appreciating it, but we have this fabulous cave system that guarantees our visitors.'

James regarded Quentin with deep, cool-blue eyes. One eyebrow raised faintly as he accepted the challenge.

'Just what is it that I wouldn't be able to appreciate?'

'Well, of course, you'd enjoy the stalactites, the stalagmites and the underground waterfall, but I was meaning that a city chap such as yourself wouldn't be able to manage the physical aspect of a trip down the caves.'

A cool laugh echoed in the kitchen.

'Maybe the farm manager would show me around,' James said teasingly.

Bubbles of anger popped and fumed in Charlie's blood. It was a pleasure to snap, 'In that suit? Don't be ridiculous.'

His cool dark-blue eyes met hers and she felt the strength of his personality like a little shock in her body. He was looking at her as if she amused him, which made her feel even more angry.

'I can change,' he said.

'You're not fit enough to manage the trip.'

'Can you manage this cave?' he asked her directly.

She lifted her chin.

'Of course.'

'Then so can I. We'll go after lunch.'

He turned back to his dinner. Charlie felt a mixture of relief and loss now that he was no longer directly looking at her. She was hot all over and her knees were trembling. And then she saw the problem with her plan. If this man was so threatening that she felt uncomfortable sitting next to him in her own kitchen, what would it be like to be alone with him in a dark cave?

'I'll phone the meteorological office,' Quentin said, going out to the phone in the hall.

'The house rule is that nobody leaves for the caves without checking the weather.'

Charlie didn't look at James as she

spoke. In her heart she was hoping for rain. But Quentin came back smiling.

'All clear,' he announced.

Charlie's heart sank. Her early-warning system was sending trickles of fear along her nervous system, but there was no help for it. She was committed.

★   ★   ★

James lounged in the messy farmyard watching Charlie wrestle with one of the tractors. She pulled her head out from under its rusty bonnet.

'It needs a new distributor cap,' she announced.

'Can I run you to a garage?' he offered politely.

Charlie laughed.

'That's where I'll go for it,' she announced, pointing to a pile of discarded farm machinery that lay in one corner.

Weeds grew up through the rusty pile, and as Charlie began to climb, she disturbed two hens who squawked as

26

they fluttered to the ground.

Loose animals, James thought. This place has got to be ripe for modernisation! He was glad he'd decided to check out the farm before making an offer. He should get it for buttons, and then clean up when the grant scheme became public.

Could he make even more money if he modernised before he sold it on? James watched Charlie's neat bottom as she grubbed around in the scrap heap. There was no chance of the farm manager co-operating, that was for sure. Better stick with what he knew best — quick purchase, and an even quicker resale.

Charlie slid down the heap clutching something that looked like a black rubber octopus. James expected her to give it to the farmhand, but she fitted it herself, and the engine roared into life. The farmhand gave a triumphant toot as the tractor rattled past James, and drove off up the rutted track.

'I'm sorry I kept you waiting,' Charlie

said, wiping her hands on an old rag. 'But we've still plenty of time for the caves. Let's go.'

'Why don't you have new machinery?' James asked, thinking of the glossy government brochures he'd been reading.

'Can't afford it,' she replied briefly. 'And a lot of the new stuff is no good on an old farm like Deepdale. Our gates are too narrow, for a start.'

James had already noticed all the stone walls.

'It would be a big job to widen those gateways,' he mused, 'but if you knocked all the walls down, you could put up wire where it was needed.'

He felt pleased with his assessment of the situation. How difficult could it be to run a farm? Then he looked at Charlie. She had seemed cool before, but the face she turned to him now was positively Arctic.

'Wire fences are ugly, unecological and dangerous,' she snapped.

Then she ducked her head as if she

intended to say no more. James looked at the small, hostile figure that strode out so freely next to him. Not a word about profit or efficiency. He was starting to get her measure.

They continued in silence. The track they were walking along climbed steadily upwards. It was rather nice to be with a woman who didn't grab at his arm or complain that he was walking too fast. James was just looking at Charlie's boots and trying to imagine her in high-heels when she came to a stop in the track.

'Do you need a rest?' he asked.

Her face was stony.

'I think we should go back. I don't want to take you caving.'

'Why the second thoughts?' James asked lightly.

Her hostility amused him. It was a new experience to be treated so coolly by a woman. He smiled. She just didn't know him, that was all. She had him all wrong. Then he felt a pang of guilt. He was planning to buy her business and change the way she did things. It was suddenly hard to meet the honesty that shone in her clear grey eyes, so he spoke quickly.

'Why change your mind now? We must be nearly at the cave.'

Defiant grey eyes met his.

'You're not properly equipped. I must have been mad to agree to this.'

'I've got a hat with a lamp on it. What more could I want?'

'Proper boots, not trainers, and a wet suit to keep you warm and dry. You'll be cold, dressed as you are.'

James looked down at his jeans and T-shirt, then he looked at Charlie.

'You're only wearing a fleece jacket,' he told her.

She was also wearing Lycra sports leggings that outlined the lovely shape of her limbs in a way that drew his eyes admiringly.

'If you're afraid to be alone with me, then you should have worn clothes that were less revealing,' he teased.

Her delicate pink lips thinned to a

tight line, but she ignored his taunt.

'It's not only your clothes. I've been thinking things over and it's madness to take a city type like you potholing. It'll be too much for you.'

James felt really annoyed.

'Do I look like a weakling? I work out, you know. Come on.'

He pushed on ahead of her, leaving her no option but to follow him. They were right on top of the moors now. A slight breeze touched James's cheek. He inhaled deeply. It smelled clean and tangy. He looked back. Deepdale Manor was a tiny dot below them. Charlie had moved ahead again. She had left the track and was leading him across a field. She stopped by a small and scraggy hawthorn tree.

'Here we are,' she said.

James looked in awe at the deep hole in the ground. The chasm was about as big as a baseball diamond, and a mountain stream bubbled up to the lip of the far side and then gushed over the edge and down into the depths in a roaring waterfall.

Charlie was making sure that protective sacks were in place around the trunk of the tree before she tied her ropes to it. As James watched the care she took, all his suspicions that she'd never go for redevelopment plans were confirmed. Again he felt that guilt as she turned to him.

'Have you ever abseiled before?' she asked.

'No,' he replied.

'This is a safety harness,' she said, showing him how to arrange the webbing straps. 'Ready?'

'Ready,' James said, but he had to swallow hard before he could force himself to follow Charlie as she slipped over the edge of the cliff.

3

Safely down, Charlie packed the ropes and abseiling equipment into her rucksack. She had to admit that James had handled the descent down the cliff wall very skilfully for a first attempt. But for some reason this made her dislike him even more!

James was now prowling around the bottom of the hole, skirting the tumbling waterfall, and pausing to run his hands over the jagged rocks of the cliff sides. The fine mist from the waterfall spray hung in the air, wetting them both. James came back to Charlie.

'I don't see any cave entrance,' he snapped. 'Is this some kind of joke?'

Charlie met his gaze and smiled sweetly.

'The joke is on you. The entrance is right behind you. You are just too ignorant to find it.'

Her stomach swooped when she saw his suppressed anger.

'There it is,' she said quickly, pointing to a narrow slit in the cliff wall. 'It's called The Letterbox, for obvious reasons, but it might just as well be called The Lobster Trap. Once we've manoeuvred into it, the narrow, twisting rock formation means that we can't turn around and come back.'

James's expression was cool and remote. He fixed on his caving helmet like a warrior going into battle.

'Who wants to come back?' he challenged her.

Once they were through the entrance, Charlie remembered how much she loved caving. She had been so busy with work around the farm, and nursing her father, that it must be nearly a year since she'd been underground. She inhaled the cool dampness of the cave air and gazed at the multi-coloured rock formations that ran like melting wax down the sides of the tunnel walls. She felt real pleasure and enjoyment as she wriggled like a worm along the wet, sandy rock floor.

She had to wait until the narrow passage opened out before she could turn to James and find out what he was feeling. As soon as it was wide enough, he wriggled up beside her. She caught a whiff of his aftershave as he tilted his head, angling his caving helmet so that the beam of light fell on the rounded rock ceiling of the cave.

'What are those markings in the rock?' he asked.

'The coiled, snail-like ones are ammonites,' Charlie said.

James reached up and gently touched one frozen, prehistoric creature. He said nothing, but Charlie could see from his rapt face that he had caught the caving bug. He looked fascinated.

They carried on through the narrow passages for another hour, then they came out into a huge cavern. Stalactites like dinosaur teeth hung from the rocky ceiling. Drops of water fell from the tip of each spike, but any sound they might have made was lost in the roar of the underground waterfall that pounded down the cavern wall and dropped into the bottomless black lake that lay below it.

'We'll stop for a rest here,' Charlie said.

James sat very close to her in the darkness.

'What makes those columns of rock grow the way they do?'

Charlie's voice was a thin thread of sound in the vast cave as she answered.

'Lime. As the water drips through the rock, it leaves a tiny deposit of lime behind it. Over the centuries, stalactites grow down from the ceiling and stalagmites grow up from the ground.'

'Centuries,' James echoed. 'Amazing.'

As he moved his head around, examining the cave, the beam of his lamp swung crazily, casting flickering shadows on to the walls.

'How far does this cave system extend?' he asked.

'Nobody knows. It hasn't been fully

explored yet, because so much of it is under water. Cave diving is terribly dangerous. People die every year while they are looking for new routes.'

She felt James shiver.

'There are bodies down here?'

'Sometimes we can't reach them.'

'We?'

'I'm a member of the cave rescue team.'

And now, Charlie thought, when she had him good and spooked, was the perfect time to carry out her plan of losing him in the dark. But plans around the kitchen table were all very well. This was reality. Would this large, capable man let her take his light away and abandon him? Not a chance.

She chewed her lip and felt silly, and even if she managed to get his light, she had a feeling that he wouldn't be lost. He'd track her by scent or follow her by sound. She cast a secret glance at his face. His dark brows were drawn, frowning, and a worried twist contorted his mouth.

Maybe claustrophobia was getting to him.

'Charlie,' he said now, his voice urgent, 'the water level is rising.'

'No!'

She gasped. Fear dried her throat and she looked around wildly.

'The level of the lake has risen several feet while we've been sitting here. I noticed a spur of rock that looked like a lion. It's completely covered now.'

Charlie examined the water levels. Water swirled around her sturdy boots. It rose over the laces, soaking the leather. Then it gushed over her ankles, wetting her socks.

'There must be a flash flood,' she cried.

James rose to his feet.

'What's the quickest way out?'

'Long Pot,' Charlie said, forgetting that the name of the exit would mean nothing to him. 'But we may not be able to use it. The low tunnel leading to it is impassable when the water rises.'

'Can we get there in time?'

Cold water gurgled up Charlie's legs, reaching her knees now. Fear put a bony hand around her throat and squeezed hard. It was hard to voice her frightening conclusion.

'No. It's too far.'

The lamp on James's helmet swung towards her, blinding her as he barked, 'Is there any other way out?'

Her legs were like rubber. Water was pouring into the cave like a monster coming to swallow them up.

'There is a closer entrance, called the Butterchurn, but it's too dangerous.'

The current of running water was tugging at their legs now, pulling them off balance.

'So is this!' James exclaimed, with the suspicion of a laugh in his voice.

He was taking charge and she was letting him. But his sharp questions were cutting through the fog of panic, helping her think clearly.

'We closed it to the public because the rock face you have to climb to get out is very unstable. Big chunks of it often break away. Below it is a very narrow, bottomless rift. If we fell in, no-one could reach us.'

'Do we have any other options?'

'The official advice, if Destiny floods, is to move to the highest point and wait there until the water goes down.'

'How long?'

'Depends on the rain. Some men were here for three days once, and they survived. Once it was a week, but they . . . '

James looked at her, calculating.

'You're shivering already. You couldn't stand a night down here, never mind longer.'

'I'm not cold,' Charlie lied, but her teeth clicked together as she spoke.

'What food do we have?' was the next question.

Charlie felt like the rankest amateur.

'A couple of bars of mint cake in my rucksack.'

James eyed the water swirling around them and came to a decision.

'We certainly wouldn't die of thirst!

But dressed as we are, and without food, we couldn't take much exposure. We'll try to get out.'

Charlie felt a flash of anger at his calm assumption of control, but at the same time, she was swinging around, leading the way to the tunnel that led to the Butterchurn. Her instincts were telling her that he'd made the right decision, and there was no time now to argue. The kind of red and white tape that road menders use was strung across the entrance to warn people away from the entrance known as the Butterchurn. They ducked under the tape and went into the narrow passage.

'Faster,' James urged.

It was becoming difficult to stand up against the force of the rushing water. Small boulders rolled treacherously underfoot. Charlie was shivering continuously. She was glad of James's warm, steadying hand supporting her from behind.

'Turn off your lamp and look up,' Charlie said.

She noticed that, because of his greater height, the water that was lapping at her armpits only reached James's waist. They both looked upwards. A pale glow seemed to take shape at the top of the cave.

'Daylight,' James exclaimed.

He made to take a step towards it, but Charlie pulled him back.

'The rock falls away here, and look how strong the current is!'

She pointed to the ominous, swirling water that was rushing into the gulf that lay under the cliff.

'It's too late to wade to the exit. The current will suck us down.'

'No, it won't. We'll swim past it on the other side.'

Charlie ducked her head.

'I can't swim.'

He regarded her incredulously.

'Can't swim?'

The scorn in his voice made her stick up her chin defiantly.

'Deepdale's nowhere near a beach, and the rivers are cold.'

'You don't have to tell me the rivers are cold. I'm standing in one!' James retorted, then his deep voice softened. 'And so are you. Charlie, you're shivering so hard it looks like a dance craze. Let's get you out of here.'

'You go,' Charlie said. 'I'll go back to the cavern, find a ledge and wait for the water to go down.'

Somehow James's laugh was no surprise.

'Abandon a damsel in distress? Give me a rope.'

Charlie unslung her rucksack and passed James a length of rope.

'I'll swim across and secure it on the other side,' James said, tying one end of the rope around his waist. 'Then you can pull yourself across.'

She expected him to plunge straight into the swirling water, but instead, he took a swift step and closed the gap between them.

'Hey,' she cried, startled, but, wet, cold lips cut her off.

As his lips moved searchingly over

43

hers, they began to warm. An answering heat rose in Charlie's body. The dangerously cold water that swirled over her was touching chest-high now, tugging at her, pulling her off balance, yet his warm hands held her safe, and Charlie pressed nearer to the magical source of heat and life and power that was so close to her.

Then sense returned, and she pulled away. She could feel her heart thumping, hear the roar of the water in her ears.

'Are you crazy? We could be killed.'

'I know,' James said ruefully. 'But if that kiss is to be my last experience on earth, Charlie, I want you to know that it was a good one!'

And then he stepped out into the treacherous water and began to swim.

Charlie's fingers pressed against her lips as she stood shivering, waiting for him to call her once the rope was fixed on the other side of the cavern. Instead, he swam back to her.

'Don't put yourself at risk!' she protested. 'I can do it alone.'

'I know you can, Charlie, but you don't have to. I'll be right behind you.'

Charlie pulled herself along the rope with white-knuckled hands, but her real support was the knowledge that the full force of James's power was behind her. With him there, it was easy to forget the danger and make her way through the water to the base of the cliff.

'I'll go first and fix a rope,' James said.

He was gone before she could stop him.

'The rock is loose,' she shouted after him. 'Test every handhold.'

A shower of rock proved her words and made her draw back. Now she was thinking of the bottomless cavern that lay below them. If he fell, it would be her fault. A lifetime passed before she heard him call.

'Get ready to catch the rope!'

She caught it, but her cold fingers fumbled over the knots. She forced herself to hurry because she thought

James might come back for her if she was having trouble. She took a deep breath before she began climbing, but it was easy with the rope. As she drew closer to the natural light, Charlie smelled the fine, warm smells of brown earth and green growing things. She was longing to reach them.

She could see James peering over the lip of the entrance. He grasped her shoulders in his strong hands. It was a sweet relief to accept his help and pull herself out of the cave.

'Thanks,' she gasped, rolling over on the grass. 'Thanks for that.'

James sat on the short, moorland turf laughing at her. Now she realised that it was raining hard. His drenched clothes clung to his body.

'You looked like a hippo emerging from a mud hole,' he gasped.

Charlie, too, needed an excuse to laugh.

'And you look like a scarecrow!' she screamed.

The high wind blew black clouds

across the sky. A lightning bolt flashed very close to them, illuminating the moors like a photographer's flash.

'We'll have to take shelter,' Charlie bawled. 'Follow me.'

4

James could feel heavy drops of water puMmelling against his skin as he followed Charlie over the darkening moor. His feet squelched in his trainers as they breasted a ridge, and then went down a slight dip. Despite all she had been through, Charlie strode out confidently. He admired her for that, and he was glad that she knew where she was going.

Charlie paused and glanced back over her shoulder, checking on him. He lifted his hand and gave her a thumbs-up. She flashed him an enchanting, dimpled smile that impacted his heart deeply. His sudden, warm feeling terrified him. It was a very long time since he'd allowed himself to feel anything for a fellow human being. It hurt too much. He was glad when Charlie stopped again, and interrupted his thoughts.

'Did you hear that?' she asked him.

James listened, but could hear nothing else but rain.

'It's an animal in distress, by the sound of it,' Charlie explained.

'Let's get on!' James said impatiently.

He was cold and his knee was hurting like crazy. He must have injured it leaving the cave. Then, very faintly, over the sounds of the storm, he heard a sheep bleating.

'It's a lamb, and I think it's in trouble,' Charlie said.

'How can you tell all that from one little bleat?'

'I just can. Help me look for it, will you?'

Charlie reached up and clicked on the caving light on her helmet. The moors seemed even darker outside the yellow circle. The wind plucked at James's clothing and battered against his body. He sighed and switched on his own lamp. He started walking next to her, turning his head this way and that, angling the beam of light over the dark moorland. They both heard a bleat coming from the left, and veered over to the source of the sound.

It was so dark, James nearly took a step out into nothingness before realising that he was standing on the edge of a sheer drop. He let out a yell as he jumped backwards.

'Charlie! Stay back!'

She halted just behind him, but then she moved forward cautiously and peered over the rim of the old quarry.

'Get back from there!' he shouted angrily. 'You could easily fall over.'

'I can see the lamb. It's stuck on a ledge halfway down.'

'OK, we found it. We'll come back for it in the morning.'

Charlie turned wide, indignant eyes on him.

'We can't leave it! It might try to escape and fall off. Sheep have no sense.'

'Neither do some humans,' James muttered, watching Charlie shaking ropes out of her rucksack. 'I'm sorry, Charlie. I refuse to go down that rope.'

'I don't want you to go down it. I want you to hold it while I go down.'

James found his hands closing on the wet rope she thrust at him, but even as he gripped it he shouted, 'Charlie! I forbid you to do this!'

She gave him a cheeky grin.

'Hold tight!' she yelled, and was gone.

James let out some slack in the rope and braced himself. How dare she defy him! The thought of Charlie putting her life at risk for a stupid animal made him grind his teeth in fury. He'd kill her when she got back!

Thunder rumbled nearby and a lightning flash lit up the moors. Rain slanted down like lines of steel knitting needles. James had a sudden, ironic picture of his usual way of spending an evening, turning over the financial papers, his computers humming from every corner, bringing news directly into his home from the world's stock

51

markets as they opened.

Not so much a home as an office extension, an inconvenient voice remarked in his head. James squashed it firmly. This was no time to start on an analysis of his life. The rain was still gushing over him as if it came out of a fire hose. He guessed that Charlie had reached the lamb.

He eased the weight off his bad knee and began pulling in the rope as she began the return journey. His angry thoughts buzzed around his head. Risking her life for a lamb! Scaling a fifty-foot cliff in the middle of a storm to rescue an animated powder puff!

Her head appeared suddenly over the rim of the quarry and she scrambled out. As soon as he knew she was safe, he attacked her, the words coming straight from his heart.

'You are the most stupid woman I know,' he howled into the wind. 'Do you realise how dangerous that was? How stupid? You risked your life for a lamb that couldn't be worth more than fifty pence frozen, and mine, I might add. Charlie, I want you to promise me that you'll never do anything so foolhardy again.'

James paused and drew in a deep breath. Charlie was kneeling at his feet, checking every inch of the lamb.

'Charlie?' he questioned.

She looked up at him.

'It seems to be all right.'

'Did you listen to a word I said?'

Charlie stood up and tucked the lamb under her arm.

'Of course I did.'

'Then what did I say?' James said, determined to stand his ground.

Rain poured over her face as she gazed up at him innocently.

'You said that I was silly to rescue this lamb.'

'I put it much more forcefully! I want you to realise that — '

'James,' Charlie interrupted, giving him a slanting look through her wet lashes, 'let's not stand out here in the

53

rain. I want to get under shelter, even if you don't!'

★ ★ ★

Charlie sat back on her heels, looked at the old fire grate and smiled. Flame licked at the crumpled-up paper. The kindling started to crackle.

'That's got it,' she exclaimed, popping the cheap, disposable lighter back into its place in a rusty tea caddy.

As bigger pieces of wood began to burn, a comforting orange glow lit the shepherd's stone cottage she and James had taken shelter in. Although the slate roof was still mostly in place, rain dripped from a few spots in the ceiling, making wet rings on the hard, earth floor. Wind blew in under the eaves, stirring the cobwebs that drifted against the walls. But a feeling of safety and shelter wrapped around her like a quilt. It was good to be indoors.

James, meanwhile, was dragging bales of straw from a polythene covered stack in one corner.

'I always wanted to make a den,' he observed, piling the blocks up to make a cosy enclosure in front of the fire. He cut one bale open and spread the fragrant golden mass on the ground for them to sit on.

'Open another one,' Charlie said. 'I want to make the lamb comfortable.'

Once she had the tiny animal settled, she went over to a blue plastic barrel that stood by an old stone sink.

'Any whisky in there?' James asked hopefully.

'Tins of milk powder and drinking chocolate,' Charlie replied.

James watched her hang a battered black kettle on a hook that pivoted over the fire.

'Prehistoric,' he breathed, shaking his head.

'It's good enough for lambing,' Charlie snapped, giving him a dirty look.

'Oh, it's five-star luxury compared to sitting out the storm in those caves,'

James said hastily. 'Charlie, will anyone be looking for us?'

She felt a pang as she admitted, 'They'll be worried, of course, but no-one could even attempt a cave rescue until the water levels drop, and we'll be back long before then.'

'I'd hate to be the object of a cave rescue,' James observed. 'Pity I left my mobile in the car. Don't you have them on the farm, Charlie?'

Stung by the criticism she read in his question, she snapped, 'The batteries are always dead just when you really need to call someone.'

Cool blue eyes met her challenge.

'Gadgets are only as smart as the people who own them. I recharge my batteries on a regular basis.'

'But your full-charged phone is in your car.'

'True.'

'Well, then,' she said triumphantly.

He lifted a sarcastic eyebrow.

'Frightened of new technology?'

Charlie didn't feel like telling him

that she had only just finished installing a state-of-the-art computer as part of her effort to make Deepdale more profitable.

'Dad said technology causes more trouble than it's worth,' she muttered.

Her voice thickened with emotion as she thought of her father.

'He used to go mad when the hands spent ages fiddling with the machines. He always threatened to go back to scythes and hand tools.'

James's head snapped towards her. His voice held surprise.

'This was your father's farm? You grew up here?'

'Yes. Why?'

'No reason,' he answered nonchalantly.

Charlie couldn't read the complex emotions flickering in his expression as he continued.

'I guess you don't feel like carrying on without him. Is that why you want to sell Deepdale?'

'I do not want to sell my home!' she exploded.

James lifted an eyebrow, encouraging her to explain. She felt a queer sense of shame as she stumbled over the painful words.

'Death taxes.'

James looked surprised.

'But didn't your father — '

He cut himself off, and Charlie knew why he'd stopped. The answer was obvious. If her father had taken care of the tax situation, James wouldn't be sitting here now. Her father had been hopeless with money, but she'd loved him, and right at this moment she hated James.

'What on earth do you want a farm for?' she spat out.

A quirk of one dark eyebrow showed that James had recognised her hostile mood, but he spoke calmly enough.

'A man can diversify, can't he?'

'Diversify from what?'

'Industrial property.'

'That tells me exactly what you do.'

'I buy any kind of rundown industrial land,' James said. 'Sometimes I sell it for housing, or a new factory. Sometimes it's more profitable to break up the business and sell off the pieces.'

'I still don't understand what you want with a farm.'

'I just felt like a change,' James said in an amiable voice.

Charlie looked at him sharply, feeling untruth in the air. There was a smile in his innocent blue eyes as he said, 'The kettle's boiling, and, if you don't mind, I'm going to take off these jeans and dry them over the fire.'

Charlie turned her back on him. Her wet clothing stuck to her coldly. After a moment's thought, she took off her fleece jacket and hung it on a rusty nail over the fireplace. The straw rustled behind her. A large pair of wet jeans appeared on the next hook over the fire.

She didn't look around, but concentrated on measuring powdered feed into a jug and mixing in the boiling water. It felt very cosy inside the wall of straw bales that enclosed them like a golden armchair. The sound of the storm outside only made their little camp seem more attractive. The lamb lifted quivering black nostrils and started bleating eagerly as the smell of hot milk filled the air.

Charlie tested a few drops of the formula on the inside of her wrist. It was cool enough, so she picked up the lamb and sat with it on her knee. It began to feed at once, happy, slurping sounds filling the air.

'His tail is rotating like an egg whisk!' James said, looking over at them with a smile. 'Charlie, did you say hot chocolate?'

He was surprisingly deft and had the enamel mugs filled in no time.

'I've found the Kendal mint cake,' he said, sitting in the straw next to her.

'You go ahead,' Charlie said, noticing that he was politely waiting for her. 'Lamb Chop will be through in a minute, and then I'll have mine.'

James bit into the sugar bar with gusto.

'Midnight feasts!' he said with relish.

'I feel like a schoolboy again.'

Perversely, Charlie wanted to needle him.

'What ho, Jeeves!' she mimicked his cut-glass accent. 'Don't tell me you're a public schoolboy.'

'Why not? What have you got against them?'

'Nothing.'

Nothing except their confident manner, Charlie amended privately. No wonder she felt James had the advantage over her. He'd been trained to act as if he had.

'Didn't you miss home?' she wondered aloud. 'School was all right, I suppose, but I could never wait to get back to Mum and Dad.'

Lost in nostalgic memories of bursting off the school bus and racing home to her smiling mother moving around the kitchen and pictures of her father grumbling over his impossibly tangled accounts, it was a moment before she realised that James was just staring into the fire.

'James?' she questioned.

He looked at her directly. The frozen pain in his expression made her feel sad for him, although he answered casually enough.

'I didn't see much of my father, and we moved a lot. School was OK.'

The bottle was half empty now. Charlie shifted Lamb Chop so that she could get a hand free and touch the only portion of James's body that she could reach — his bare foot. She patted it sympathetically.

'What about your mother?'

The foot under her hand jerked a little, telling a truer story than the smooth voice.

'I don't remember her really. She divorced Father and went to live in the United States.'

Charlie shuddered at this bleak picture of his childhood. She wasn't surprised when straw dropped all around them as James stood up.

'More hot chocolate?' he questioned, in a tone that made it clear the subject of his childhood was closed.

While James clanked the kettle against the tin mugs, Charlie eased a very full, sleepy lamb into the straw nest she had made for it. As she turned towards James to take her mug of hot chocolate, she saw how awkwardly he was moving. She could see black bruises forming and swelling.

'That knee's giving you trouble,' she observed. 'Let me have a look.'

'It'll keep till the morning,' he said hurriedly.

'Don't be so macho,' she chided. 'It might need bathing.'

Laughter lit up James's blue eyes.

'I don't need any more water on me tonight,' he said firmly.

Charlie couldn't help smiling, but she persisted.

'If there's dirt in it you might get an infection. Let me have a quick look.'

James muttered under his breath, but he sat down and let Charlie angle his bruised leg towards the firelight so that she could examine it.

'How did you hurt it?' she asked gently.

Warm breath touched her forehead as he answered.

'Would you believe, I don't know?'

Charlie's heart was moving a little too fast. She was used to tending farm injuries, but for some reason, looking at James's leg was making her feel strange. She stole a glance at his face. His thick black hair was drying to a glossy raven's wing. Stubble shadowed his strong chin. The tightness in her chest increased as she met the blueness of his eyes. It was an effort to keep her voice steady.

'I don't think there's any real damage. It's very swollen, of course, and it will be painful to walk on, but . . . '

Her fingers drifted away from his injured knee as awareness flashed between them. Panic clutched at her throat, but she was aware of a surge of primitive excitement. Straw rustled beneath him as James shifted his weight. The clean golden scent of the straw floated up towards Charlie as she took a deep, unsteady breath.

James lifted one hand and touched the fair strands that fell over Charlie's forehead. He twisted one curl around his finger. The gentle intimacy of his touch was unsettling, yet there was a sweetness in it, too. His eyes met hers with a knowledge and an authority that took her breath away.

Charlie dropped her gaze and took refuge in the rôle of nurse.

'There's a bottle of embrocation in the stores. I'll rub some on for you so you can walk in the morning. It's about three miles to Rafferty's farm.'

She felt as if she were running away as she left the warm spot by the fire to get the small, glass bottle. James was watching her with a mixture of hunger and admiration that made her nervous. She took refuge in briskness.

'Yes, well, let's get this knee seen to, shall we?'

'Yes, nurse,' James said.

He spoke gravely, but there was a smile in his eyes. Charlie flushed, but forced herself to concentrate on the injured knee. It suddenly occurred to her that it was her fault he was injured because she had lured him into the caves. She felt horribly guilty. She shook the embrocation bottle vigorously and took off the cap. James wrinkled his nose as the smell hit him.

'What is that stuff?'

'Lanolin, mainly. The farmhands use it all the time.'

Charlie poured some liquid into her hands, set the bottle on the ground, then rubbed her hands together to warm the lotion. James tensed as she touched him, and then relaxed as he felt the gentleness of her touch.

'That feels better,' he admitted.

Charlie felt him relax back into the straw. If only she could be as relaxed about their situation. It was an effort to keep her hands steady, to keep their motion to a smooth, steady glide as she gently massaged in the embrocation.

Was she the only one who was affected like this, she wondered suddenly. Was James aware of the tension between them? Did he know how he was affecting her?

James swallowed hard as he tried to control himself. He looked up at the cobwebby rafters of the old barn, but he couldn't banish the image of Charlie's fair head bowed over his knee. He gave up and looked back at her.

He could just see the curve of her cheeks and her gold-tipped lashes. Her plait had fallen over one shoulder. As her gentle hands slid over his bruised knee, it was an effort not to let his eyes linger on her.

Did she know what she was doing to him, he wondered. What a complex woman she was. She appeared so tough and macho in her rôle as farm manager, yet she had looked like a Madonna as she tended the orphaned lamb, and the gentle sensuality of her touch as she tended his hurt knee was driving him crazy.

Don't mix business and pleasure, he told himself. Charlie is not the kind of woman who'd take an affair lightly, and she's going to go crazy when she finds how you're going to renovate Deepdale.

He wished the farm hadn't been her family home. He always tried to avoid the messy, human, personal issues. He felt his insides squirm as he tried to imagine blowing off Charlie with a redundancy package. Maybe he could set her up with a market garden or a flower shop? James smiled. He liked the idea of helping her, being her business manager, seeing more of her.

He looked back at her. The log fire cast dancing shadows on her face. Her smooth skin was lightly tanned to the colour of a nice brown speckled egg. Her lubricated hands slid over the skin of his knee in a delicious flow. She was unique, wholesome and totally desirable. He felt his resolve melt.

'Charlie,' he said softly.

She looked up, and her eyes darkened with startled awareness as they met the desire in his.

'You must know how beautiful you are,' he said.

Her thick lashes swept down and he saw with disbelief that she was blushing. Her shyness only made him want her more. Outside the building, the storm rampaged. Inside their straw nest in the firelight it was like being enclosed in the glowing bubble of a Christmas tree decoration.

Very slowly, James drew her into the circle of his arms. She fitted into them as if she was designed for him. She felt soft there, sweet and very pliable. James kissed the hollow under her ear, marvelling at the silk of her skin, the sweet, feminine scent that clung to her hair.

She trembled as she felt the touch of his lips, and James continued to kiss her softly along the hollow of her throat. When he felt her relax and surrender to him, he put his lips close to her ear.

'Kiss me back,' he whispered.

He was aware of the muscled

perfection of her body as she twisted in his arms. This is how a woman should feel, James thought triumphantly, as he captured Charlie's lips with his own. He took her face in his hands and tilted it up towards his, deepening the kiss. Her response was innocent and whole-hearted. Then, cutting through his sensual daze came the awareness that something was wrong.

'Charlie, wait!' he groaned.

'James,' she breathed softly, lifting her head to look up at him.

The sight of her sweetly-flushed face so close to his made James forget why he'd stopped kissing her. There was a drowsy sensual contentment in her eyes. He pressed a light finger on her lips.

'Oh, Charlie,' he said, and kissed her again, only to be disturbed by a nibbling at his toes!

He yelled out loud. Charlie shook herself, seemed to come out of her sensual dream, and joined James in looking down at his feet. There in the straw below them, sucking hard on James's big toe, tail going like a propeller and a blissful expression on his face, was Lamb Chop!

Charlie screamed with laughter and fell back in the straw, rolling with glee. James couldn't repress a smile as he detached the lamb from his feet and popped it back in its nest. He was feeling so happy that he wasn't prepared for Charlie's reaction when he held open his arms for her to come back to him.

'No,' she said, shaking her head and regarding him with serious eyes. 'It was a moment of madness, a reaction to the caves. Let's just forget it, OK?'

James felt like a footballer being shown the red card.

'You can't stop me now! This is more than a reaction, and you know it. You can't deny that there's an attraction between us'

Charlie pushed an errant wisp of hair off her brow.

'I wasn't thinking. James, we'll be

working together if you buy Deepdale. We should keep our relationship professional. You'll be my boss.'

'Then do as I tell you. Come here!'

Charlie regarded him with steady, honest eyes.

'What would an affair do to our working relationship? What would happen if it finished?'

James hunted for something glib and easy to say, something that would get Charlie back into his arms and kissing him again as quickly as possible. But he ran into problems at once. He couldn't say in honesty that he was planning to stay for ever and farm Deepdale Manor in the traditional fashion, because he found that he couldn't look into her eyes and lie to her.

He couldn't tell her that they wouldn't be working together for long. He couldn't tell her that, when the grant money was publicly announced, he was going to raze her family home and plant whatever crop was being subsidised that year before selling it at a vast profit. He was lost for words.

'Close your mouth,' Charlie advised tartly. 'You look like a goldfish.'

Moving briskly, she built up the fire for the night. She burrowed into the straw a distance away from him and deliberately turned her back to him.

'Let's get some sleep. We must get down to Rafferty's farm before anyone has the chance to send a search party out for us in the morning.'

She seemed to fall asleep instantly. Her breathing grew soft and heavy as James watched her. Gradually he regained control of his feelings. She was right. It would be madness to get involved. He settled himself into the straw.

He yawned, and realised that he had a clear view of the sleeping Charlie. The soft firelight rendered her face shadowed and vulnerable. Her thick lashes lay on her cheeks like those of a china doll. Her lips screwed up in a baby pout that James found completely adorable.

'Steady on, Thornton!' he told

himself. 'Don't go soppy on me now. You are going soft!'

But he felt well on it! James had always wanted to go camping. The open fire smelled delicious, just as he'd always dreamed it would. But a chill crept up from the earth, and although the side of his body near the fire was toasted, his other side was cold. James pulled up some more straw and winced as the sharp blades pierced his skin. And yet, he'd never been so happy in his life.

As his thoughts fragmented towards sleep, he tried to puzzle out why he felt so great. An image of Charlie's sleeping face floated into his mind. Angry, he pushed it aside. No way was James Thornton affected by a female. Determined to assert his everyday personality, he groped for the person he felt he normally was, find the reactions he should really have.

Lamb Chop snuffled, and bleated softly in his sleep. James found the appropriate response for a mature, London property dealer when faced with a small white lamb.

'Mint sauce!' he muttered sleepily.

But there was a smile on his lips as he drifted off to sleep, and all night through. His body was turned to face Charlie, as if to protect her. He slept so soundly that he wasn't aware of the storm blowing itself out over the moors.

At dawn, Charlie had to shake him hard before he was awake enough to tackle the walk down to Rafferty's farm.

5

Charlie came back from telephoning home to Martha to find the kitchen of Quentin Rafferty's farm filled with tension.

'Martha said she wasn't worried about us at all,' she announced, eyeing the two men curiously.

Quentin sat by his kitchen table looking like a hunched, defensive vulture. James towered over him, looking furious.

'I could overlook my own involvement in this,' James was saying, 'but what I can't forgive is you putting Charlie's life at risk.'

'My life at risk?' Charlie questioned. 'What's going on here?'

James threw a folded newspaper on top of the unwashed dishes that littered the table.

'Ask Quentin why he hid the weather report from you, and why he lied about his telephone call to the met office.'

Quentin hunched a shoulder against James and whined.

'Oh, stop making such a fuss! You're both all right, aren't you?'

'A fuss!' James exploded.

Contempt sharpened his tone.

'You put Charlie's life in danger! And for what?'

Understanding flooded his face and he continued.

'I'll bet you wanted to buy Deepdale yourself, at a lower price than I'm prepared to pay. Am I right?'

Quentin shifted uneasily and kept his eyes on the floor. James regarded him with withering contempt.

'What kind of a man would send a woman into danger because he wanted to make a profit?'

'A modern man,' Quentin muttered. 'You don't know as much as you think you do. Charlie's my fiancée, and she doesn't need looking after.'

Charlie stared at Quentin in disbelief. Why was he laying claim to her now? She admitted that at one time she'd thought . . . but he'd always been so evasive, so reluctant to commit himself, that she'd given up on thinking of him that way long ago.

James spoke very softly.

'If Charlie is considering linking up with a man who'd treat her the way you seem to believe is OK, then I'd say she needs looking after more than she thinks she does. Women should be protected, cherished, not put in danger for profit.'

The impact of James's words hit home. Charlie considered the way he'd rescued her, a stranger. He'd taken over the situation and protected her. He hadn't considered leaving her for a second. He'd treated her the way a knight would treat his lady. And she knew now that she could never settle for anything less. Just as she opened her mouth to deny her engagement to Quentin, he spoke again.

'Charlie doesn't need cherishing.'

'Yes, she does,' James said stubbornly. 'All women do.'

Quentin's mouth twisted in a sulky pout.

'Don't you talk to me about fragile, little women. The whole plan to get you down the caves and abandon you there was Charlie's! She wanted to frighten you away.'

James swung on Charlie with eyes that blazed under his black brows.

'Is that true?'

Her mouth was dry.

'Yes,' she admitted, 'but — '

James cut her dead.

'Then you'll make a lovely pair. I wish you the joy of each other.'

Stung, Charlie attempted to defend herself.

'What was I supposed to do?' she demanded. 'What would you do if your family farm was threatened?'

A hard lump rose in her throat as she continued.

'I love Deepdale. I'd do anything to save it from a ruthless shark like you.'

'So I see,' James said softly. 'But calling me ruthless is the pot calling the kettle black. Your actions were hardly innocent.'

'I didn't know about the storm,' she reminded him. 'And I'm not ruthless, not the way you are.'

'How would you describe yourself?'

'I was just being defensive, protecting my rights.'

His blue eyes swept over her face, examining every tiny reaction.

'Would you really have left me down there?'

Despite herself, she had to smile, remembering the moment when she'd realised how unrealistic her plan was.

'How would I have taken your light away?'

A reluctant smile curved his lips.

'A masterly plan, but some problems with the execution then?'

'And you liked caving,' she reminded him, chuckling. 'You weren't claustrophobic a bit! And I only ever wanted to scare you off.'

His smile reached his eyes this time.

'Oh, Charlie! Let's call a truce here. Shall we just say that we're both determined people?'

She nodded, liking the easy way he'd put the matter aside, forgiven her for a trick that could have ended so badly. Quentin, on the other hand, she despised. She swung around to confront him.

'Why did you lie about the flood warnings?' she demanded, but she was speaking into an empty kitchen.

While she and James had been absorbed in each other, Quentin had seized the opportunity to flee from a man who had every good reason to want to punch him.

'Never mind him,' James said. 'Let's get back to Deepdale.'

'Martha will be preparing a feast,' Charlie told him. 'I was to ask you if you wanted ham or bacon or sausages. Then there's mushrooms, tomatoes, fried bread, eggs, baked beans and black pudding. Oh, and cereal or toast and marmalade, if you prefer it. What would you like?'

'Everything,' James said, following her out into the rainwashed splendour of the still-early morning. 'And gallons of black coffee to follow.'

He turned his head and looked down at her with a query in his eyes.

'It certainly smells fresher out here. If ever a kitchen needed a wife, that one did. Charlie, are you really engaged to Quentin?'

She glanced at him quickly, then looked away again.

'No,' she said firmly, knowing that it was true.

Nothing in the world would induce her to marry Quentin now.

James continued to inspect her.

'Be careful,' he warned. 'He means to have you as well as the farm.'

Charlie shook her head, not sure what she was trying to express.

'Oh, I don't blame him,' James said, very quietly. 'I want you myself.'

Startled, she looked up and met his

eyes. Sparks seemed to fly from them as their gaze connected. It was an effort to keep her voice steady.

'We already agreed that it was madness to mix business and pleasure.'

A shadow seemed to dim the blueness of James's eyes as he registered her rejection. He persisted no further.

'That's right,' he said mildly, 'so we did.'

He seemed to shake himself and resume his normal air of command.

'Then, as our host seems to have no intention of running us home, I suggest we make full speed for Martha's breakfast.'

★   ★   ★

Despite the pain in his bruised knee, James found himself singing in the shower. Martha's breakfast had been food for the gods and he was feeling extraordinarily well, if somewhat sleepy. He stepped out of the shower and helped himself to a clean, fluffy towel from a pile on top of a wicker basket.

As he dried himself, he looked around the room with pleasure. He had to admit that Charlie had fitted out the rooms beautifully. The heavy, old-fashioned, wooden furniture, the white-washed walls and the polished floor spoke eloquently of the farmhouse's past, but the bed inside the brass bedstead was a well-sprung divan. There was a generously-sized central heating radiator and the bathroom was fitted up to the highest modern standards.

Yes, she'd done a good job, James decided, admiring the matching patterns of the curtains and bedding. He guessed that the mixture of nostalgia and comfort would prove very attractive to guests. He'd only had time for a quick glance over the farm books so far, but it seemed to him that the bed-and-breakfast side of Deepdale was making more profit than some of the farming activities.

Once he was dry, he wrapped another towel around his lean hips and sprawled on the bed. He clicked open his briefcase and dug out his mobile phone. He lay back in snowy white pillows and chalked up another good mark for Charlie. The pillows were soft, but supportive, and the bed beneath him was warm and comfortable. He stifled a yawn. Too comfortable. He was still missing half a night's sleep, but he had things to see to.

It took him a couple of hours to run through his normal business, and by then, his subconscious had obviously come to a decision. James always trusted his inner feelings in matters of whether to move ahead with a deal or not. He made a quick call to his broker and then his bank, making sure that he had enough liquid funds to cover the price of Deepdale.

Then he called the York firm of solicitors acting as executors of Mr Hargreaves' estate. They protested over the lowness of his offer, but he pointed out that it was a cash price for a quick sale. Then he left them to think over the advantages of an immediate sale.

He lay back on the bed and yawned again. He felt the surging sense of pleasure and satisfaction that always came to him when a business deal was going his way. He picked up his mobile again. Should he call his current lady friend, Sabrina? He had to concentrate hard to conjure up a picture of her face in his mind, which was odd, because her stunning looks had taken her to the very top of the modelling profession.

His fingers paused over the buttons of the phone. In fact, now he thought of it, their last date had been another disappointment. He had managed to book a table at a restaurant run by the latest celebrity TV chef.

The food had been marvellous, the guy deserved every flicker of his two stars, but Sabrina had picked at everything disdainfully, whining that the food was too rich, and she couldn't afford to put on weight. She had smoked foul-smelling French cigarettes the whole evening, ignoring the smothered coughs from the people who were unfortunate enough to be dining near them.

With a feeling of relief that he didn't pause to analyse, James remembered that she had told him something about being away in New York modelling that week, or possibly Paris. At any rate, there was no need to call her. James slipped his phone into its charger with a smile. He lay back on the bed and burrowed into its comfort, closing his eyes for a minute . . .

Judging from the delicious smells, dinner was going to be ready soon after he woke up. Remembering that Martha had told him there was a special dinner party that night for a group of history enthusiasts, all lecturers from a local university, James brushed his hair and dressed smartly before going downstairs.

A burst of laughter told him that the paying guests were in the lounge, so he passed it by. Opening the next door cautiously, he found an empty dining-room. The polished priory table was set with silver and sparkling crystal in readiness for the evening. He admired Charlie's efficiency, and wondered where she was.

As he entered the kitchen, Martha turned a flushed face over her shoulder.

'Charlie's ironing napkins in the utility room, if you're looking for her.'

'I wasn't looking for her,' James denied.

Martha gave him a look that said she wasn't fooled.

'What's the point in fighting it?' she demanded. 'Two young things like yourselves. It's only natural.'

'But I wasn't looking for Charlie.'

James suddenly laughed at his own foolishness.

'Well, maybe I was. But it's no good, you know, Martha. Business and pleasure don't mix.'

Martha finished what she was doing and came quickly over to the kitchen table. She counted out a cut-glass bowl for each guest, and began scooping measures of delicious-looking home-made gooseberry fool into the pretty glass containers.

'You can garnish them for me,' she said, thrusting a plate covered in frosted mint leaves at James. 'One candied violet and two leaves for each.'

James picked up one of the tiny sweets in his large hand and carefully garnished a pudding.

'That's right,' Martha said approvingly, 'but you're wrong about not mixing business and pleasure. Why shouldn't they go together?'

James glanced up at her sharp, birdlike eyes, taken aback at her bluntness. Snugly ensconced in this farmhouse kitchen, engaged in his homely task, it was difficult to explain the cut-throat rules of the business world.

'Office politics lead to trouble,' he mumbled. 'It can get messy, complicated.'

'Life is messy,' Martha retorted, 'and none the worse for that. What's office politics, if it's not people working together? And if you're working together, what's wrong with loving the person you're working with? Farms like this one thrive on teamwork. Deepdale was founded on love. Two centuries ago, a rich wool merchant fell in love with a pretty farm lass. He built the manor for her, and they lived here happily for over fifty years.'

James politely suppressed a smile at the innocent simplicity of the old woman's vision. Modern life is nothing like that, he told himself. And then he was surprised by a pang of longing deep in his heart.

'If only it was,' he muttered.

He felt a deep, elemental yearning for the serenity of a life like the one Martha had described — a man and a woman who loved each other, working side by side over the years.

One of the doors into the kitchen flew open, and Charlie entered on a waft of freshly-ironed cotton. Her arms were full of pink linen squares.

'Hello, James,' she said. 'Do you know how to fold a water-lily table napkin?'

He didn't, but he followed her into the dining-room and hung around, watching her fold napkins with dizzying speed and put the finishing touches to the table. As he watched, he became increasingly aware of just how gorgeous Charlie was looking this evening.

She was wearing a simple black dress, but she needed nothing else with that knockout figure of hers. James just kept finding more and more to admire. Elegant heels showed off the length of her muscled but very feminine legs. Her long fair hair had been swept up on top of her head.

She had neat, little shells for ears, and her only jewellery, small pearl earrings, gleamed impeccably on her pink lobes. He wondered how she could look so feminine. Only yesterday, he'd seen her mend a tractor, yet her hands were well cared for, and a discreet nail varnish glowed on the tips of her fingers.

As she moved lightly around the room, a waft of light, sexy perfume touched James's nostrils. It aroused his senses, teasing and tantalising him. He couldn't take his eyes off Charlie as she stood at the head of the table.

'That's everything,' she decided, with a satisfied nod of her head. 'We can call them in.'

'Just a minute, Charlie,' James said.

He wanted her to himself for a few minutes longer.

'You look fabulous tonight. You could hold your own with any city socialite.'

Charlie looked at him with something less than pleasure in her clear eyes.

'You sound surprised. Do you think that I'm such a country bumpkin that I go to parties in my overalls?'

He moved forward quickly, anxious to undo the harm that his thoughtless words had caused.

'No, that isn't what I thought at all! It's just that, well, you're so groomed, so elegant. You take my breath away, and all this for a party of strangers. It's good of you to go to so much trouble, Charlie.'

Now he saw a shadow of guilt in the honest grey of her eyes, and a tinge of tell-tale pink stained her cheeks.

'They told me it was a very special occasion,' she mumbled, but James felt hope kindle in his heart.

He had moved so close to her that all he had to do was reach out his arms and he was holding her fragrant body by the upper arms.

'Tell me the truth,' he demanded. 'Was it for me?'

She looked at the floor, and the pink flush became a betraying flood of red.

'Good,' James said softly. 'I'm glad you wanted to look nice for me.'

The warmth and the perfume of her body was reaching out to him, driving him crazy. He tightened the grip on her arms, drawing her close.

'Look at me, Charlie,' he said softly.

She kept her head down, and he moved even closer, watching the betrayingly fast rise and fall of her breathing, letting his lips just trail across her cheek to her earlobe. He opened his mouth to whisper soft encouragement to her, but the dining-room door banged open.

'I say!' a voice hooted that was trained to fill a lecture hall. 'Did you say dinner was at eight o'clock? We're all simply starving!'

Charlie sprang away from James and looked at the carriage clock on the mantelpiece. Three minutes to the hour!

'I was just about to call you,' she assured the hungry academic.

James watched regretfully as Charlie recovered her composure and turned into the perfect hostess. It was ridiculous, but he felt jealous of the care and attention she lavished on her guests. As he watched her make sure the party went with a swing, he marvelled at his own possessiveness. He'd never had such a strong urge to sweep a woman away and have her all to himself.

At first, as Charlie laughed and chattered, he suspected that she was trying to make him jealous. But then he watched more closely. He saw how professionally she was behaving, and he knew that she was just making sure that all her guests, male and female, had an evening to remember. It was her job, he reminded himself, practically grinding his teeth as he watched her being charming to a bearded man who taught history.

She had to make sure they had a good time. Then they would come again and recommend the farm to all their friends. But, confound it, did she have to keep tilting her head back and laughing at the fellow's jokes?

James kept his expression light, and joined in with the general fun of the evening, but inside, he was a tumbling mass of conflicting emotions. New, painful, disturbing sensations surged up inside him in a way that he found unsettling.

He made the effort and subdued his confusing feelings. His original instincts had been right. Stay cool, don't get involved, a quick sale, a tidy profit, and a clean getaway.

He'd done it many times before. Why should this deal be any different?

6

The next morning, James felt decidedly grumpy when he didn't see Charlie at breakfast.

'I need to see her,' he explained to Martha. 'I wanted to ask her if I could use her office.'

Martha gave a sharp look.

'She thought you might. She told me to show you where you could plug in your laptop.'

Defeated, James followed Martha to the office. It had once been the library of the manor house. Brown leather chairs were grouped in front of the fireplace, dusky, velvet curtains framed the two sets of french windows, and the rows of bookshelves seemed to contain equal numbers of well-thumbed paper backs, gilt-bound classics and text books about farming.

James softened when he saw the

evidence that Charlie had thought about him. She'd cleared a space for him to work, and a Thermos flask of coffee sat on a silver tray.

'You won't be disturbed,' Martha said, slipping out and closing the door behind her.

James sat down, but a scratch at the door disturbed him. It was Bingo, demanding admittance. He got up and let in the little Jack Russell. Then he couldn't resist having a snoop around Charlie's domain, picking things up and putting them down again.

He was interested to see a clear line between the scruffy, yellowing piles of books and ledgers that Mr Hargreaves used to run Deepdale's business affairs, and the state-of-the-art computer that must be Charlie's. A pile of brand new software and training manuals told him that she was putting all the farm accounts on to the most modern of systems.

He got a strange sensation in his heart when he thought how wasted her gallant efforts were going to be. Everything would change when Deepdale was razed in order to claim government grants.

Amongst the gilt-framed oil paintings and wall-mounted guns and fishing rods were a number of silver-mounted framed photographs. James's gaze skimmed lightly over the many images of a smiling couple who were obviously Charlie's parents. When he came to a photograph of a smiling child on a barrel-shaped pony, his attention sharpened, and he took the picture off the wall in order to examine it more closely. Charlie had the same happy smile as her parents and was obviously enjoying every second of her life. He put the photo back, but couldn't resist looking at some more.

Pain lanced at James's heart as he compared the bleak vista of a boarding school where nobody ever visited him with the tight, loving family that surrounded Charlie's every move. There were her parents smiling at the play school, at the gymkhana, at a picnic on the moors. There was a happy, glowing, sunny Charlie in her school uniform, in her jeans, in a summer dress. He saw with a shock that the last picture was dated only a year ago.

Poor Charlie. There was a sadness and a maturity in her eyes now that hadn't been present in the photographs of her as a child. She'd had to grow up since her father died. And she'd done it magnificently, James thought before he could stop himself. Although one could see traces of the carefree child she had been, she was a lovely, gracious woman now, one that any man would be proud to —

He broke off his dangerous thoughts with a snap. He opened his briefcase and got out his laptop computer, pushing aside the coffee tray as he did. He couldn't afford to be softened by these sweet, domestic touches. His way of getting through life was simply not to feel, not to get involved, not to trust anybody, because then you couldn't get hurt. Work was all the fulfilment he needed.

Charlie had paid extra to have the fastest connection on the internet. It was easy for him to hook up with his colleagues in New York and Tokyo, Buenos Aires and Sydney. James worked for several hours, completely absorbed, although at some level, he was aware of the comfortable feel of a warm dog sleeping on his feet.

When the market closed in Hong Kong, he pushed back his chair and flung his hands up in the air yawning widely. His mouth was dry. He unscrewed the Thermos. The coffee was hot and fragrant. He took a refreshing sip and reflected on how splendidly the morning had gone. Bingo must have brought him luck. He'd made a fine profit, and completely forgotten that he'd been up here in Yorkshire rather than in London. A good phone line was all that mattered these days.

A tap on the door was followed by

Harry Pickles' eccentric smile. James noticed that he wore a tea cosy hat even indoors.

'Come in,' James invited.

'Hi, boss,' Harry said.

'So, you're talking to me today?' James teased.

Harry had the grace to look shame-faced.

'That were before I knew you,' he explained.

James felt he had been offered a genuine apology.

'Forget it,' he offered, and the old man gave him a sunny smile.

'Going in to Appledale,' he said. 'Have you seen it yet?'

'No,' James said doubtfully. 'Is it worth seeing? How big is it?'

The old man shrugged.

'Big enough. Got a dentist. Charlie's taking me for me new teeth.'

'I think I'd better come along and check out the town,' James said, then seeing the amusement in Harry's eyes, he added, 'nearby facilities can really affect the price of a property.'

'Oh, aye,' Harry said, but his old blue eyes were sparkling, and James felt he hadn't fooled him a bit.

The door opened again, and Charlie stuck her head in.

'Is Harry in here? Oh, there you are, Harry. I'm ready to go.'

James felt his lips twitch as he looked at her. She was so obviously regretting the feminine impulse that had led her to dress up for him the night before. She was wearing army boots, baggy khaki pants, a shapeless, old sweater, not a scrap of make-up, and a tightly scraped-back plait.

She was absolutely gorgeous, James thought. Nothing could hide her glowing youth, the sheer vitality of her being. I'd want her if she was dressed in an old sack, he decided, but it was clear that she didn't feel the same way about him.

The temperature of her clear grey eyes was set at cold enough to chill, but when Harry turned to her and said cheerfully, 'James is coming with us,' she became even colder.

'You're welcome to a free ride,' she snapped in glacial tones. 'There is absolutely no need to ask me first. Just assume that I'll take you any time.'

James switched off his computer and tidied away a few papers before deciding to take her sarcastic speech at face value.

'That's very kind of you,' he said, beaming.

She glared at him for a few seconds more before hissing like a cobra with hay fever, turning on her heel and stalking out. Harry gave James a conspiratorial nudge in the ribs.

'Women!' he whispered. 'She's acting mad because she wants you to kiss her, but she don't like to admit it.'

'You think that's it?' James enquired, amused by the old man's shrewd perception of the affair. 'She's going a funny way about it if she wants me to kiss her!'

'You take no notice of the way she's

acting,' the old man insisted. 'Don't let it put you off her. She's a lot to worry on just now, but she's the sweetest-natured woman in Yorkshire.'

James smiled to himself as he followed the old man out of the room. Harry's fears that he'd be put off were unfounded. Given his normal taste in women it was hard to believe, but he found Charlie with her deliberately concealing clothes and her frosty touch-me-not manner the most amazing challenge he'd ever encountered. No woman had ever interested him half as much as this one.

Outside Deepdale Manor, Charlie stood bareheaded in the light rain that was falling and kicked the gravel as she waited for Harry and James to join her. She didn't want to go anywhere with James. She never wanted to see him again, let alone take him shopping. When the two men finally emerged, she got into the driver's side of her battered Land-Rover and slammed the door.

'We'll take mine if you like,' James

offered, putting his head in through the missing window on the passenger side and looking at the hard bench seat next to her.

'You do what you like,' Charlie said through tight lips. 'I'm going to town under my own steam.'

Sighing, James opened the door and slid along the seat to make room for Harry. Charlie set off with a jerk. She drove much faster than usual down the rutted track that joined Deepdale to the main road.

'Stop!' James shouted.

Charlie screeched to a halt and turned to him. She could hear her anger turning her voice into a harsh croak.

'Too rough for you?' she enquired.

But James wasn't looking at her. He was gazing off over the green slope of the fields.

'Isn't that Sam?' he snapped abruptly.

Charlie followed his gaze. The farm-hand, Sam, was driving a tractor up the hillside. It was loaded with bales of hay for the sheep.

'Yes. So what?'

James swung a furious glance at her.

'I'm going to stop him!' he announced.

Harry took one look at his face and slid out of the way. James jumped out of the Land-Rover and stood on one of the stone walls that bounded the field. He put his fingers to his mouth. The resulting whistle was so loud that, against all odds, Sam heard him over the noise of the tractor engine and looked around.

James motioned Sam to stop, then jumped over the wall and started running towards the tractor. Charlie gathered her startled wits, leaped out of the Land-Rover, jumped over the wall and started running after James. She was absolutely furious at his calm assumption of authority. How dare he tell her staff what to do?

James had a head start on her. By the time she reached him, he'd already switched off the tractor engine and pocketed the keys.

'What on earth are you doing?' Charlie exploded.

James swung eyes that were equally full of anger towards her.

'I could ask you the same thing. Do you realise that this tractor hasn't got a roll bar?'

Charlie faltered, realising that it was true. Sam was not driving one of their newer vehicles, but the old model that all the farm staff called Old Faithful. It was kept as a standby for emergencies. It should have been scrapped years ago, of course, but amazingly, Old Faithful started every time, so they kept using it on the odd occasion.

'Sam?' she questioned. 'What's happening?'

'The other one wouldn't start,' Sam explained. 'I thought I'd get sheep fed and then have a tinker with it.'

'You have to be alive to tinker with anything,' James cut in. 'The ground is still wet after the storm. What if you rolled over? Without a safety bar, you could be crushed under the tractor. It's not only stupid, it's illegal, isn't it?'

He swung round on Charlie.

'Don't you take health and safety measures around here?'

Conflict raged in Charlie's breast. She knew he was right. But she was also furious at the way he had taken command. He was running her business, her life, and her heart, like a steam roller, and the knowledge enraged her,

'Of course we do,' she replied haughtily. 'All the other tractors are safe. It's only this old one, and we only use it occasionally.'

James gave her a look that was so full of scathing contempt that she was cut to the quick.

'And what if it only occasionally kills someone?' he growled.

Charlie bit her lip and tried to control her bitter resentment. Who did he think he was, turning up here and trying to change everything, finding fault with the way she did things?

'Dad used to use Old faithful all the time,' she fired at him. 'He wasn't a slave to all these stupid, petty-fogging regulations.'

'Petty-fogging!' James repeated. 'I think I hear a quote there, Charlie. It doesn't sound like your sort of vocabulary. Nevertheless, I do take health and safety seriously.'

He turned to the farmhand.

'Sam, I'm giving you back the keys, but I want your solemn word that you will drive carefully back to the yard, taking no risks whatsoever, and that you will never again go anywhere on this farm in a tractor that has not been fitted with a safety roll bar.'

His gaze turned on Charlie, waiting to see how she would react. The words to countermand that order trembled on Charlie's lips. She had never wanted anything so much as to defy this hateful, maddening, infuriating man who stood on the wet grass next to her, coolly ordering her staff around and looking at her with a mocking amusement that was almost harder to bear than being found in the wrong.

But, to be fair, Charlie knew that he was absolutely right. There was no way she would buy a new tractor without modern safety precautions, or let any of the staff drive one. But they had all got so used to Old Faithful it had never occurred to them that it was dangerous. But she had to admit that it was. Shame washed over her. She had been busy, but she could have found time to see to it.

'Go on, Sam,' she said and out of the corner of her eye she saw James relax, as if he'd been expecting her to fight him. 'James is right. We'll get the garage to weld a bar on. Don't use it again until it's been fixed.'

Sam started the engine and drove off very slowly. Charlie and James started back to the car. Harry, Charlie saw, was sitting on the stone wall, watching them as if he was at the theatre.

'Thank you, Charlie, for backing me up there,' James said softly.

She had to swallow hard. Fury still burned inside her. The fact that James was going to be the boss around here was beginning to sink into her brain. Her tangle of feelings choked her. Oh, part of her wanted to acknowledge that he'd been right and she'd been wrong, but the way he'd gone about it maddened her, issuing orders all without a trace of by-your-leave.

'You're the boss,' she snapped, 'or at least, that's what you tell me,'

To her horror a rush of tears blurred her vision and thickened her voice.

'We employees have to do what we're told,' she finished.

They had reached the stone wall. Harry had vanished. James stopped before scrambling over and said to her, his voice curiously gentle, 'Do you mind so much, Charlie, if it's me who buys your farm?'

She didn't look at him. She scaled the wall and jumped down the other side. Harry was lurking by the Land-Rover. To her fury, he waved James into the vehicle first, and then bundled in, taking up a lot of room, so that Charlie found James sitting so close to her that her hand brushed against his leg every time she had to change gear.

The well-known route to Appledale had never seemed to take so long. Every time the side of her hand touched the warm, hard muscle of his leg, chills and thrills of excitement pulsed through her. She was so glad to draw up in the market place and leap out.

'I'll meet you back here at two o'clock,' she said.

Harry ambled off through the rain, on his way to the dentist, but James came slowly round the Land-Rover. She was trying, with trembling fingers, to lock the driver's door. The lock had always been tricky, but today it simply would not lock. James towered above her, his silent pressure unnerving Charlie to the extent that she gave up. There wasn't much car theft in Appledale, she told herself, shoving the keys in her pocket.

'You never answered my question, Charlie,' he said.

She looked around her at the lovely, but damp, cobbled market square, as if inspiration would strike her from the clock tower, or rescue come riding up out of the pens where the weekly livestock auction was held. There was no help anywhere, so she was forced to look back at James.

The challenge in his blue eyes was like a blow. It left her feeling breathless. It was an effort to summon up the necessary defiance. She smiled at him as sweetly as she could.

'I'm a professional farm manager, Mr Thornton, and that means that I pride myself on my ability to get along with the management.'

A new shade entered the blueness of his eyes, a warm, tempting, alluring shade.

'Oh, Charlie,' he groaned. 'We could get along so well. I can't stop thinking how it felt to kiss you, and it makes me want more. So much more.'

His arms came out to hold her. Charlie was trapped against the side of her Land-Rover. She couldn't escape. She didn't want to escape. His lips came down on hers in a hard, possessive move that sent her senses reeling. Her reservations shattered as she felt herself soften and go boneless, melting into the strength of his body.

James lifted his head and traced the progress of a raindrop down her cheek with gentle fingers.

'I'll never go out in the rain without thinking of you,' he promised softly.

Charlie snuggled blissfully into the warmth of his body. She felt safe, protected, infinitely cherished and special. She lifted her head and met the melting tenderness of his look.

'But you're getting so wet,' she protested.

'Don't care,' James said, before bending his head to kiss her again.

The rain seemed to fall harder, and wetter! James lifted his head.

'Well, maybe I do,' he said, laughing

down at her, rain dewing his lashes.

He looked around him. At the end of the square was a black and white coaching inn. Hanging baskets full of bright flowers soaked up the spring rain, and the gilt of the namesake Golden Lion was polished until it gleamed.

'Let's go in there,' James said, taking Charlie's hand and tugging her in the direction of the hotel. 'We'll book in for lunch. It'll give us a chance to get to know each other better over a nice, intimate meal.'

Charlie felt the cold of the damp air against her skin like a wet flannel as she emerged out of the shelter of James's arms.

'Are you crazy? The whole town would be gossiping about us in seconds.'

'So what?' James enquired softly. 'Let everyone know what good terms you are on with the new management! It won't do your status any harm.'

Charlie was shaken in so many

directions at once that she hardly knew where to start putting him right. She couldn't be sure of his intentions but she couldn't help thinking that, with encouragement, he would be quite happy to take their friendship a step further.

'You're off your trolley if you think Appledale is the sort of place where people curry favour with the boss's current lady friend,' she said furiously.

James had the grace to look shame-faced.

'I didn't mean that the way it came out,' he protested. 'I'm sorry if I'm giving you the wrong impression. My intentions are entirely honourable!'

Charlie faced him angrily, hot words boiling on her lips. She didn't know what infuriated her more — the knowledge that he had power over her feelings or the knowledge that he had power over her life. She had better control herself and make sure that he affected her as little as possible. She gritted her teeth.

'I am going to do my shopping now, if that's all right with you, boss.'

James stepped back as if to let her go, but he was watching her intently, and as she brushed by him he spoke softly.

'You'd better get used to it, Charlie, because your coldness and your silly clothes aren't putting me off a bit. There's an attraction between us that can't be denied.'

She swung back to him and lifted her chin.

'There may be a kind of animal attraction, but that's all it is, physical, and I don't intend to give way to it again.'

James came closer and the nearness of his body and the intent expression in his blue eyes made her knees tremble beneath her.

'Why not?' he enquired. 'I like it, and I think you do, too, if you'll only admit the truth. Why deny ourselves a bit of fun?'

'Fun!' Charlie said bitterly.

'You were enjoying it a few minutes ago.'

Rain was running down her face. It was cool against her heated cheeks, and she hoped it was hiding the angry tears that slid down her wet skin. She spoke slowly, as if it was important to make him understand.

'A few minutes ago I was forgetting that I would be putting my home and my career at risk for this so-called fun. I've come to my senses now. It will never happen again. We must not become involved.'

And, clutching her shopping basket as if it were a shield, she stalked off into the market square.

7

James watched Charlie's retreating
back. He was surprised when she
paused and came back to him. There
was such painful honesty in her eyes
that he instinctively put out a hand to
comfort her.

'I'm sorry if I encouraged you,' she
said stiffly. 'I was carried away.'

Then she swung on her heel and
walked into the baker's shop, her back
ramrod straight.

James admired the truth in her. She
hadn't blamed it all on him. She had
honestly acknowledged that she, too,
had felt the magic between them and
been swept up in it. Because she'd been
so honest, James was forced to consider
his own behaviour with equal clarity,
and what he saw there didn't make him
proud.

I just wanted her, he admitted to

himself with a sigh. I didn't pause to consider that Charlie isn't the sort of woman to go for a casual fling. I should have known better.

As he wandered around the old town, finding, somewhat to his surprise, that he was easily able to purchase everything on his shopping list, James continued to chew over the question of why he had behaved so wildly. It had been a crazy thing to do. But Charlie drove him crazy! She affected him like no other woman, and he just didn't know what to do about it.

The last shop he entered was an outdoor pursuits shop. It smelled deliciously of leather and waxed jackets. James had only meant to buy wellington boots to combat the wet weather, but so enticing were the goods on display, that he ended up buying a whole country outfit.

'I'll wear them, now,' he said impulsively.

He felt strange as he walked out of the shop, dressed in green corduroy trousers and a new waxed jacket, but Harry, who was waiting outside, whistled in admiration and walked around James slowly.

'Proper country gent,' he said in satisfaction.

'I feel like I'm in fancy dress,' James admitted, stretching out a leg and looking at his new leather boots and thick socks.

Harry shook his head.

'You suits it,' he announced firmly. 'It's like you was born to county life.'

'To Deepdale Manor born,' James joked, smiling, but feeling warmth around his heart.

It was nice to think of belonging somewhere.

'Come on, Harry,' he said, 'I'll treat you to lunch. Where's the best place?'

Without hesitation, Harry led James into the Golden Lion.

'Harry, love,' a nice, matronly-looking woman called. 'How nice to see you! And your friend. Will Charlie be joining you? I saw her getting out of the

Land-Rover earlier.'

'I somehow don't think she will,' James replied.

From the curiosity in the woman's eyes, James concluded that she'd seen them kissing next to the Land-Rover. Charlie had been right. He'd been a double fool to think that the local hotel was a good place for a private tryst in a small, gossipy town.

Harry contented himself with giving James a sharp glance as they sat at a table for two in the window. He didn't ask any awkward questions. He set out to entertain James with stories of the countryside, and to such good purpose that James couldn't remember the last time he'd had such an enjoyable lunch.

'That was the best steak and kidney pie I've ever tasted,' he told the waitress as she cleared up. 'Would you like another pint, Harry?'

The tea cosy hat shook.

'One's enough, but they do right good puddings here.'

James took the hint and ordered

them both a sweet. Harry beamed approvingly.

'That's handsome of you,' he said.

Then he leaned forward. The earnest expression in his eyes warned James that something important was forthcoming.

'I tell the what, lad,' Harry said, his accent becoming more broad as he became emotional. 'I'll take thee on t'churchyard after dinner. I'll show thee the wife's grave.'

'Thank you,' James said.

It was one of the strangest privileges he'd ever been offered, but he was astute enough to recognise that he'd been granted a great favour.

'Were you married for long?'

'Fifty year,' Harry said.

Sticky treacle toffee pudding with butterscotch sauce arrived at the table and the old man attacked it with gusto.

'A man ought to be married.'

James was surprised.

'You're in favour of marriage?'

'Oh, aye. A man's no good without a

woman behind him. And a woman needs a man. Take Charlie. She's been in need of a husband for a while, but there weren't no-one good enough locally.'

James steered the conversation into safer channels.

'Where did you get married?' he asked.

'In church where she's buried,' Harry said. 'Where else?'

Where else indeed, James reflected, thinking of impersonal registry offices and people scouting around for a church that was smart enough for their wedding.

'I suppose you were christened there and went to Sunday school, too?'

Harry nodded.

'It's right bonny,' he said proudly. 'Sup up, and I'll show thee round it.'

James thought of the stability of Harry's existence. An emotion stirred in him that was unfamiliar at first, and then he recognised it — jealousy. He couldn't imagine such continuity. He looked up at the old man, who had got to his feet by the table. Harry's eyes met his with such open friendliness and goodwill, that a second, unfamiliar emotion attacked James. His conscience was pricking him. Would Harry be so friendly if he knew James's true plans for Deepdale?

Meanwhile, Charlie's mood was not improved when she called in at the outdoor pursuits shop. Maureen, an old school friend who worked there, approached her at the speed of light.

'Charlie!' she screamed. 'Who is that man who's staying with you? He's one to die for!'

'His name is James Thornton,' Charlie said shortly.

'I want to marry him and have his children,' Maureen exclaimed.

'He's some kind of rat from the city,' Charlie snapped. 'I thought you wanted to marry a farmer.'

'I changed my mind.' Maureen sighed. 'And he'd make a gorgeous farmer. He looks so handsome in green.

Oh, Charlie, I sold him some boots! I kneeled at his feet. Bliss! I could have stayed there for ever.'

'Prince Charming is supposed to kneel at Cinderella's feet,' Charlie pointed out unkindly.

Maureen was undaunted.

'A new twist on an old tale. Oh, Charlie, is he really staying with you? You have to invite me over. Tell me all about him. I'm serious. This is it! This is love. Mrs James Thornton, that's me!'

'Oh, there's no sense to be got out of you today,' Charlie snapped. 'I'll see you next week, Maureen.'

Then she softened. She'd known Maureen a long time.

'You're welcome at Deepdale whenever you like, you know that.'

'I'll be there!' Maureen promised fervently. 'I'm just going to get my hair done, and I'll be there. Do you think he likes brunettes? Shall I go auburn? What shall I wear? Charlie, come back! Do you want to be my bridesmaid? Charlie . . . '

Charlie escaped with relief into the drizzle still falling. What had got into Maureen? James was nothing special. Her mood wasn't improved on finding that, although it was quarter past two, neither Harry nor James was back. She waited for them outside, leaning on the Land-Rover bonnet getting wet, cursing them for being late.

When they finally appeared she took a second look at James. He was wearing his new clothes, and she saw with a shock that they suited him. His big, well-muscled body looked at home in the sturdy, sensible clothes of the country. He looked chunky, handsome, devastating.

I want to marry him and have his children, Charlie thought. It just popped out before she could stop herself. She was horrified. She tried to joke herself out of it. You're getting like Maureen, she told herself. Crush of the month, that's all it is. A handsome face and a few kisses. What do they amount to? Nothing!

Time seemed to stretched out as

James walked towards her over the wet cobbles of the market square. Diamonds of rain hung in the thick black of his hair. He was giving Harry his full attention, and Charlie was able to drink her fill of him.

Be careful, Charlie she warned herself. You can't afford to give in to these feelings. The way he strode along as if he owned the place was attractive, but there was a warning there, too. She wrestled with her unruly heart and by the time the two men reached the vehicle she had herself pretty much under control. She drove all the way back to Deepdale without saying a word, but to her intense irritation, the two men didn't seem to notice. They were chatting about pest control, and she heard Harry offering to take James out shooting.

Since when have they been such good friends, she thought crossly, screeching to a halt on the gravel sweep outside Deepdale. Martha was standing by the door with a plastic raincoat over her head. She paused for a moment to watch them arrive.

'I'm just going out to the deep freeze,' she called. 'What do you fancy for dinner, James?'

James, James, James, Charlie thought crossly. What had got into everyone? They were falling like ninepins before him!

Over the next few days, she had to admit that he seemed to fit effortlessly into the life at Deepdale. He wandered all over the farm, with his devoted slave, Bingo, trotting behind him, entering measurements and notes into a tiny computer that didn't look big enough to be serious. In some mysterious fashion, he always seemed to be around just when one needed help, but, unlike the farmhands, Charlie resisted the temptation to ask for his help or advice. She wasn't falling for his charm, even if everyone else was.

'Don't you need to get back to London?' she spat at him crossly one warm day.

The air was humid after all the recent rain. Big grey clouds hung over the farmyard, getting lower and lower. She had a delivery to get under cover before the threatened rain arrived.

James shook his head.

'Not until I've helped you unload these sacks of fertiliser.'

A teasing light shone in the blue eyes.

'I don't need help, thank you. I can manage.'

'I know you can, but it will take you twice as long if you do it all by yourself.'

This was so undeniably true that Charlie said no more. I don't have to talk to him while we're working, she thought furiously, avoiding his gaze. He could shift two sacks to every one of hers. She tried to speed up, determined not to be beaten by a city man, but with an amused twist to his lips, James worked even faster, keeping pace with her easily. The sacks were shifted in less than thirty minutes.

'Thank you,' Charlie said stiffly,

hoping that James would go away now, but he just gave her an enchanting grin and perched himself on top of the pile of sacks.

'Have a drink,' he offered, holding out a bottle of mineral water.

She was too thirsty to refuse. The cold water splashed over her mouth and lips in a refreshing cascade.

'Thanks,' she said briefly, wiping the mouth of the bottle and handing it back to him.

James was regarding her with an intent gaze.

'You look so appealing when you drink,' he said quietly.

Charlie's whole body jerked.

'Don't start that again!' she snapped, looking away.

'Why not? Don't you like me?'

She was determined not to meet the passion she knew was flaring in his eyes. She didn't look up.

'No,' she replied, looking at the ground. 'I don't like you.'

Heavy, warm raindrops splashed on

to the ground as the promised rain arrived. She could smell the wet dust. James's voice was soft and there was a smile in it.

'Oh, Charlie, and after I shifted all those sacks for the love of you.'

'You wasted your time.'

Again, there was a soft laugh in his voice.

'And I hate wasting time. Tell me, what I can do to please you?'

His voice was temptation. Charlie nearly yielded to the soft bliss of a man who seemed to be offering so much. But then she caught herself sharply. Don't give in to that attraction. It was strong, admittedly, and seemed to be growing as the days passed. But there was no future in it. James was going to be her boss. He had made her no promises, and if it all went wrong, she was the one who would have to leave Deepdale, and that would break her heart.

A wave of pure, molten fury surged through her. She turned on James as ferociously as a wild cat.

'If you want to please me you can get out of my life!' she exploded. 'You think you can shift a few sacks and impress me? You fool! You're buying my farm. How could I ever like you?'

James fell back a step. His eyes met hers in a long gaze. The rain fell around them, hissing and splashing. Neither of them noticed it. James's voice sounded shaken.

'I see. I didn't realise you felt so violently with me, Charlie.'

There were iron nails in her throat, making her voice a rough whisper.

'Deepdale is my home, James. Can't you see what you're threatening? Doesn't the word home mean anything to you?'

She raised her blurred gaze to his face. His blue eyes were distant, thoughtful, as he replied.

'It never did before. I never had a home, Charlie, but I think I'm starting to see what I missed out on.'

She didn't want to cry in front of

134

him, but it was becoming harder and harder to control herself. She couldn't stand to be near him a second longer. Charlie whirled around and raced across the farmyard, making for the secret childhood place she had always gone to shed tears — the hayloft.

James watched her shaking back retreating across the yard through the now heavy curtain of rain, and shook his head in dismay.

'Losing your touch with the women, Thornton,' he remarked sarcastically to himself.

For a moment he thought about going after her. Seeing Charlie cry had affected him deeply. He longed to comfort her, but his commonsense told him that, at this moment, following her would only make things worse.

He'd have to stop thinking about her. The memory of those eyes with tears clinging to the lashes made him feel so bad. He couldn't stand thinking about it. He'd think about business instead.

James drew a letter from his solicitors

out of his pocket. He ducked under shelter to read it through once more. He'd meant to consult Charlie about it. Apparently, one of the farms that bordered Deepdale was encroaching on to this property.

His lawyer had pointed out that, without any sort of formal agreement being in place, the neighbours seemed to be pasturing a whole herd of cattle on Deepdale's land. He'd check it out, James decided. Anything was better than hanging around the farmyard, wondering if he dare go and comfort Charlie. He strode off on a tour of inspection.

James wanted to be very sure there was no mistake, so he measured and re-measured the boundary several times. The two fields in question ran down to the Tarmac road on the very edge of the property. The rain had stopped, but big clouds still raced over a dark sky. James leaned on the stone wall and went over all the figures again. There was no doubt that the neighbours were encroaching.

A large, expensive car pulled up on the steaming Tarmac of the road, so silently that James didn't hear it at first.

'I say,' a loud plummy voice hooted, 'you there. Are we on the right road for Appledale?'

James looked over the wall at the fat owner of the condescending voice in astonishment, then understanding. They thought he was a farmhand! The warm feeling of belonging made him feel light-hearted.

'Oi'm not rightly sure,' he said, not caring that his attempt at a rustic accent came from the other end of the country, if anywhere! 'Oi don't go there right often. But I hear tell as how there be a big town down that road!'

The flashy car slid away. James could see the driver shaking his head. James shook his own head. What had got into him? He hadn't played such a prank since his schooldays! He was a grown man now. It was time he got back to business. James looked at the situation and made a decision.

The neighbour's cows had followed him into the corner of the field and were standing around watching him as if they were glad of the company. As soon as he got back to the house, he was going to insist that either they were removed, or a grazing fee be paid. Why not move them now, while down here?

He looked at the now sunny fields. There was a large hole in one section of the wall that divided the two fields. A few makeshift hurdles were strung across it. James took them down. He walked over the gap, and all the cattle meekly followed him back on to their own land.

James put the hurdles back, smiling to himself. Farming was easy when you knew how. It was fun, too. A decision crystallised in his mind. He was going to live in the country. With the profit from Deepdale, he would buy a cottage, or a nice little house, on the outskirts of Appledale, maybe.

Feeling pleased with himself, James strolled back to the house. The phone message awaiting him there made his smile even broader. He was humming a tune as he showered, changed, and set off in his Range Rover in the direction of York.

★ ★ ★

Charlie was feeling crosser than she could ever remember feeling with old Harry Pickles as they walked back to the house at midday.

'I can't see why you all keep harping on about how wonderful James Thornton is,' she complained. 'He's a city man! He knows nothing about the countryside.'

'He's right quick on uptake,' Harry pointed out, undaunted. 'He listens to what you say, aye, and he learns from it, too. Maybe we could learn something from him. He's a good businessman, and farming is a business these days.'

Charlie kicked a stone in the path. Even though she was starving, Charlie decided that she'd better have something light and cooling for lunch. Perhaps it would help her temper. She found Martha waiting at the open door of Deepdale Manor, looking agitated.

'The police have been on the phone,' she called. 'Shackleton's cattle are all out on the road and there's already been one accident.'

★   ★   ★

A fine spring moon was sailing over the deepening indigo sky by the time Charlie heard the crunch of gravel under the wheels of James's returning Range Rover. She rose from her seat on the doorstep to greet him.

'Waiting for me?' he asked, in a surprised tone of voice.

'Yes, actually, I was. I have something to say to you in private.'

'Not a nice something, by the sound of it,' James teased.

Even now, warmed by her fury, Charlie felt the pull of attraction. She stamped on it ruthlessly.

'Where have you been?' she demanded furiously.

James's brows drew together at her tone, but he answered her calmly enough.

'To sign the papers.' He smiled. 'Congratulate me, Charlie. I now officially own Deepdale Manor!'

She turned her head aside, shaken. She'd known it was coming, of course, but now it was real. She pushed aside the implications, to think about later. For now, boss or not, she had a few words to say to James Thornton.

'Was it really you,' she demanded, her voice shaking as she thought of the worrying afternoon she had just been through, 'who drove Shackleton's cattle out of the bottom pasture?'

'Yes,' James said, 'and out they will stay until I get a grazing fee. I don't allow squatters as a matter of principle, not on my land.'

The lightness of his tone tore away the last shreds of doubt Charlie might had had about the rightness of lecturing her boss.

'You fool!' she snapped. 'Papers don't prove anything. This isn't the city. We're a community here, James. People help each other out without needing a signed contract beforehand. There's a wall fallen down on Mr Shackleton's land. I told him he could keep his cattle in our field until it was safe to send them back.'

'How was I to know that?' James demanded.

Charlie's tone was scornful, but even now, she didn't really mean the viciousness of her words.

'You could have tried asking me.'

It was hard to see his face in the darkness of the spring evening. The same damp breeze that was patting Charlie's cheek was lifting his hair, revealing a strong brow, strong and handsome. Her knees began to shake. It isn't love, Charlie thought desperately. It's anger. I'm angry with him, that's all.

'You weren't talking to me at the time,' James reminded her. 'But all the same, I'm sorry.'

Charlie knew she was being unfair, but the urge to hurt him, to slash and to claw was too strong.

'Sorry won't bring back a good cow.'

James swung on her, his big, dark outline above her stirring primitive instincts as his hands bit into her soft forearms. His voice was tense, urgent.

'How many were killed?'

'None,' Charlie had to admit, 'but the car was damaged.'

He relaxed.

'Telling me where I've gone wrong is one thing, Charlie, and I admire your courage in facing me. But tormenting me is another matter entirely. Don't do it.'

Oh, she hated him, hated the way he made her feel.

'I'll do what I like!' she said rashly. 'You don't know how I feel about Deepdale, about the country, about animals.'

She had to stop in order to choke down the painful sob that threatened to escape from her throat. She turned her head aside and finished on a broken whisper.

'You don't know how I feel about anything.'

The words vanished quietly into the night.

'Oh, don't I?' James cried, and the rough sound of his voice told her that his feelings had finally broken through his shell. 'I know how you feel better than you do yourself,' he told her, catching her chin with hard fingers and forcing her to look at him.

Moonlight spilled on to his face, turning it into a thing of sharp angles and dark shadows.

'I know that you want me and I know that you're fighting it.'

'I hate you,' she spat out, hardly able to control the trembling in her stomach and the weakness of her knees.

He drew her closer.

'Liar,' he said softly. 'You want me

just the same way that I want you. Admit it, Charlie. Say that you want me. Give me the gift of your love.'

It was an effort to speak over the thunder of the blood that was pulsing in her ears, but Charlie strengthened herself against his insistence, moistened her lips and breathed the lying words into the moonlight.

'I don't want you.'

He pulled away from her. His eyes were dark, his vibrant voice iron-hard and insistent.

'What do you want, Charlie?'

Her eyes slid away from the demand in his. Even in the dim, silvered moonlight, it was hard to meet his expression.

'I want my home,' she said.

As she spoke, she knew that the words were no longer exactly true, that her feelings had been changed in some measure by the presence of this hot-blooded male. Her words were the soft plea of a child.

'I want my home. I want everything

to be exactly the way it used to be.'

'You lie,' he growled and his arms came out to hold her.

His lips met hers, strong, possessive, demanding. Charlie tottered under the onslaught, not just of his touch, but also the truth of her own feelings. When James broke the contact and pushed her away, she staggered back, reeling. She stood in the dim moonlight, her heart racing, her life changed by the knowledge that raced through her veins. She did want this man. She wanted him more than she would have believed it was possible to want a human being. She wanted him more than anything else the world had to offer, including Deepdale Manor.

Charlie stood still, shocked by her silent admission. Her eyes lifted as of themselves and locked on to James's.

'Tell me, Charlie,' he demanded once more. 'Tell me the truth about how you feel about me.'

Charlie never knew what she would have answered him, for now several things happened at once. Lights snapped on all over Deepdale, the hard yellow beams dispelling the moonlight and passion. A blue flashing light appeared at the end of the driveway as a police Land-Rover began bumping slowly up the rutted track.

The front door was flung wide open and Martha appeared, calling out in a worried tone, 'Charlie, are you there, Charlie? You'll have to come at once. They're calling out the cave rescue. There's children in the caves. There's a whole coach party down there. And they're only ten years old.'

8

The rendezvous point was miles from Deepdale manor, where the Destiny Caves opened out into the hillside. The opening was quite spectacular, and people liked to picnic there. Farther inside, the cave system branched off into many tunnels.

Warning notices at the entrance told people not to wander in too far, and Charlie herself had placed red and white barriers about two hundred yards inside, but the school party had ignored them. A large school bus was parked by the side of the roadway, ominously empty.

'How many are down there?' Charlie asked through dry lips.

'We don't know exactly,' the leader of the cave rescue operation said, his gaze resting on a dishevelled figure. 'She's too upset to be accurate.'

A woman, quite inappropriately dressed in a light dress, and high-heeled sandals, was huddled under a blanket, crying. Her hair fell over her face and she reached up with shaking hands to push it away.

'It was so dark,' she gasped, between sobs. 'I never knew it could be so dark in there.'

Another woman, in the uniform of a paramedic, had her arms around the weeping teacher. She spoke to her calmly.

'You're safe now. It's all over. You don't have to worry any more.'

'The children,' the teacher gasped, then she broke down again as she thought of her charges. 'Oh, the children!'

A uniformed policeman strode up.

'We've found the coach driver,' he said in disgust. 'He was propping up the bar in the local pub! Anyway, he was able to give us the numbers.'

The crowd was getting larger by the second as the word spread around the district. More police, the fire brigade, another ambulance, many local farmers and all the members of the cave rescue team had appeared. A hot-dog van rolled up and some elderly ladies jumped out and began brewing up vast urns of tea. Charlie saw Martha among them, but the leader of the rescue was calling for everyone's attention.

'We now know that there is one more teacher, an adult male, still down below there.'

He paused, looking grave.

'With him are twenty-seven children, all from the city. It seems that they'd been on a trip to the York museums, and decided to stop at the caves, on a whim. They are not dressed or equipped for underground. The party started out with a couple of torches, not meaning to go far, took a wrong turn and then the lights failed. They became separated in the dark.'

His gaze then rested compassionately for a moment on the shocked and weeping teacher.

'This lady managed to keep three of the children with her. After wandering for what she estimates to be several hours, they found their way out and raised the alarm. Is the initial situation clear to everyone?'

Charlie swallowed hard at the picture the briefing conjured up. Twenty-seven children! She pushed away distressing pictures of how they must be feeling. It was best for everyone to keep calm.

The leader of the team went on with his briefing, splitting the searchers into teams, pairing ordinary volunteers with the more experienced members, making sure that everyone understood which section they were searching and what the communication signals were. As he gave the signal for the search to get under way, Charlie saw that James was shaking hands with a climber she knew slightly from the next village.

She ran over to him. A television van had joined the throng. A reporter tried to stop her, looking for someone to interview. Charlie ducked to one side and grabbed James's arm.

'You can't go underground!' she gasped.

He gave her a cool look.

'Why not?'

Because I don't want you to, her heart cried, but she said, 'Because you've no experience.'

He gave her a shrug that dismissed her.

'I didn't hear you complaining last time.'

It was so true. Charlie gave a defeated sigh and admitted the truth.

'I know you're competent, James, but you truly haven't had much experience, and I'll worry about you.'

His eyes softened, and he gave her a devastating smile.

'I'll remind you, later, that you said that, Charlie. But for now, has it occurred to you that I might not like you going down there?'

She stared at him, astonished.

'But I'm a trained member of the cave rescue!'

James gave her a rueful smile.

'You also bring out all the protective instincts in me. You're small and soft and delightfully female, Charlie. I hate to think of you in those cold, dark caves! Don't go!'

'I have to,' she said.

His eyes held hers a moment longer.

'So do I.'

'I tell you what. I'll stay up here in safety — '

Charlie gave a sigh of relief.

'But only if you will,' he finished.

She felt outmanoeuvred.

'The children . . . '

'Exactly,' James interrupted, as his partner called to him.

But James stood looking at Charlie a moment longer. His eyes met hers, asking her a question, asking her if she understood. She nodded, and he lifted his hand in salute.

'See you later,' he whispered, and he was gone.

Charlie wished fiercely that they had been paired together. She saw so clearly now that they belonged together. It was a shock and a revelation to her. It was a relief when she and her partner were called to the entrance of the cave. The rescue co-ordinator waved them off.

'Good luck, Charlie,' he shouted.

Four hours later, she thought his blessing had come true.

'Twenty-seven kids,' the cave rescue leader cried as they all were reunited on the hillside. 'And one teacher. Folks, I'd like to thank you all very, very much. We have a result here!'

Everyone screamed and yelled, letting off their feelings now the danger was over. Martha and her friends did a brisk business at the hamburger van. The fire engine bumped its way back on to the road and then off in the direction of Appledale. Tired farmers yawned and drove away.

'Why don't you get off home, Charlie?' Martha said, handing her a steaming hot chocolate. 'There's no need for you to hang around.'

Charlie sipped at the sweet, hot

chocolate. It was welcome and warming in the cold, night air. Her bones were still cold after the hours she'd spent underground.

'I'm on my way,' she promised. 'I'll just hang on for James, and then it's me for my bed.'

Yawning, feeling the adrenaline leaking out of her system now that the danger to the children was over, she stood on the dewy grass and watched people pack up. More and more vehicles bumped away over the tracks. The children had long been whisked off to hospital. They had all been suffering from shock and exposure, but Charlie thanked God that not one of them had been seriously hurt. It could have so easily ended in disaster!

A thin streak of grey lay along the rim of the horizon. The air was becoming fresher and sweeter with the promise of dawn. The crowd was really thin by now, and she was surprised she couldn't see James. She caught sight of his partner.

'Just a minute,' she called. 'Where's James?'

'He came out with me.'

'Then where is he?'

'I don't know,' the reply came. 'I hope the fool hasn't gone back down there.'

'Why would he do that?' Charlie asked fearfully.

'Well, he told me he thought he heard a cry, but just then the signal was given that everyone was found, so I signalled him to come out with me.'

'Well, one ought to follow procedure,' Charlie said. 'But didn't you report the cry to the team leader?'

The other man looked uncomfortable.

'What was the point? We had all the children. I told James to forget it.'

A cold certainty was clawing at Charlie's heart.

'James doesn't just forget things,' she said. 'If he suspected there was a child down there . . . '

She began to run towards the small

knot of people still standing by the cave mouth, all who were left of the rescuers.

'But we got them all,' James's partner protested, running behind her.

'How far do you trust that particular school party's organisation?' Charlie questioned bitterly.

The team leader looked thoughtful when the situation was explained to him by Charlie.

'We got the numbers from the coach driver,' he said thoughtfully, 'but he wasn't all that reliable.'

He looked at Charlie.

'Do you trust this guy? What's his name? James. Do you trust his judgement.'

She swallowed. Her words were a defiant statement.

'With my life,' she answered.

Oh, James, she thought, as the rescue leader called back those few who were still within earshot. I would trust you with my life, my heart, my happiness. And now you're missing! It was as if the truth was being unveiled to her at last.

She loved James — and now he was missing!

Her heart was heavy as she joined in the preparations to go underground once more, but then the team leader gave a shout.

'There's a light coming,' he yelled.

Charlie saw the kind of yellow light that was cast by the caving helmet appearing at the back of one of the tunnels. She dropped the rope she'd been coiling and ran towards it. The light got stronger. She could see the size of the man who carried it, and she recognised the massive outline of the man that she loved.

'James!' she cried. 'Oh, James! James! James!'

She hit him at chest level, laughing, crying, scolding.

'How could you go down there without me? You fool! I thought you were dead! How could you be so stupid? Oh, James, I love you so much,' she exclaimed.

'Steady on!' came the sound of his

welcome rich voice. 'Just let me hand over my little frog.'

Charlie lifted her head to look at him through her swimming tears.

'Frog?' she questioned, baffled. 'You found a frog?'

James's laugh boomed through the caves.

'I certainly did.'

He opened the puffy jerkin he was wearing, and Charlie saw to her amazement that a scrap of a young boy was clinging to James's hip.

'Meet Jeremiah Prince,' James announced, 'known to one and all as Froggie.'

'I can walk now,' Froggie announced, completely unfazed by the ring of onlookers.

James let the lad go and he stood up proudly on his spindly legs. Charlie got a lump in her throat at the boy's vulnerability, not that Froggie seemed aware of it.

'I'm mega hungry,' he informed the group of rescuers.

The team leader grinned at him happily.

'Walk this way, Master Prince,' he said. 'We just might be able to find you a hamburger.'

'You can call me Froggie if you like,' the youngster said.

Although he was easily the smallest of the children who had been rescued, he appeared to be the least affected by his experience. He didn't seemed shocked at all.

'What about James?' he enquired, twisting his head over his shoulder. 'He deserves a hamburger. He rescued me.'

Then he noticed the weeping Charlie, who was still holding James tight.

'Oh, sloppy stuff,' he announced, and tugged at the hand of the cave leader. 'Let's go eat without him. He'll probably be a while.'

James's arms were full of the laughing, crying Charlie. It would take him a lifetime to express all his feelings, and he wanted that lifetime with Charlie. He wanted the sense of permanence and belonging that he'd been missing all his life. He held her close and hugged her to him.

He had a sudden vision of Charlie, standing in an open doorway, greeting him after a long day. He decided that he'd devote his life to making her happy.

'Sorry to interrupt!' the cave rescue leader said, smiling, 'but I can't go home until everyone's gone.'

Charlie drew back out of James's arms, but she kept her hand tight in his, as if she were afraid that he'd vanish if she let him go.

'Sorry,' she sniffed, wiping her eyes.

'It's been a long, emotional night,' the leader said.

James took the Land-Rover keys from Charlie and insisted on driving her home. Sunrise lit the sky as they travelled along the country lanes. His heart was full of warmth. Of all the women in the world, it was Charlie who sat next to him, looking sleepy, but content. Every now and then she threw him a smile, a smile that made him long to take her in his arms.

They arrived back at the manor house at the same time as the paper boy on his bicycle.

'I didn't know you could get deliveries this far out!' James exclaimed.

Charlie threw him an amused glance.

'You make it sound as if we live in the back of beyond!' she commented, but there was no real venom in her voice, and the teasing smile in her eyes was so warm that James melted.

Bingo lifted a sleepy head out of his basket by the stove as they entered the kitchen. He decided there was no need to move, and went back to sleep again.

'Are you hungry?' Charlie asked, throwing the papers on the table. 'I could murder a bacon roll.'

James felt his mouth water.

'Good idea! But I'll be cook.'

In the end, they split the cooking between them. It took a long time because every time Charlie bent over the frying pan, James couldn't resist putting his arms around her and kissing her neck.

'You smell better than the bacon,' he teased.

'I think that's the nicest thing you've ever said to me!' Charlie commented, slipping out of his grasp and swiftly slicing wholemeal bread.

'I intend to spend the whole of my life saying nice things to you,' James promised, shaking dry some lettuce and arranging sliced tomato on the sandwiches.

James watched her small white teeth as they bit into her sandwich and felt almost faint with his love for her.

I'm going to ask her to marry me, he thought. Marriage would be for ever with a woman like Charlie. For ever! He took a deep breath. A minute, he promised himself. I'll just take a minute, and then I'll ask her.

Charlie yawned widely and pushed her plate aside.

'I don't think it's worth going to bed,' she observed. 'I'll just have a strong coffee and then there's a broken gate I must see to.'

James watched her with devotion as she idly picked up the farming newspaper.

I will love her for ever, he thought, and he opened his mouth, the feeling inside him now as if he were a surfer who had just caught a wave, a great, glorious, shining wall of water that would support him and carry him and take him through life to where he wanted to go.

'Charlie,' he said, 'will you marry me?'

Her fair head was bent over the paper in stunned immobility.

'I know it's a shock to you,' he said, smiling, 'but I know you won't settle for less, and I figure it's about time I settled down.'

His voice trailed off as she lifted her head to look at him. The utter fury and contempt that blazed out of her eyes made him realise that they had never really been arguing before. All her coldness, all her dislike, they had been little snowflakes of hostility compared with the howling storm of her feelings now. She was looking at him as if he'd taken her most treasured possessions and dropped them down a well, James thought uneasily. Wasn't she a bit impressed by the compliment he'd just paid her?

She placed the paper carefully on the kitchen table in front of him and pointed at the headline with a finger that shook. James only needed to see the word 'Euro-grant' to know that she now understood his plans completely.

'I wish I'd told you sooner,' he admitted honestly. 'But I knew you'd be upset.'

He gave her a smile, reaching out for her, trying to charm her, and wondering why he felt like a heel underneath.

'I was hoping that once we were married, you'd come around to my way of thinking.'

Her face was so white and stunned that it scared him.

'Charlie? This isn't a good time to think about plans for Deepdale. We'll talk about it tomorrow.'

He tried a winning smile again, but his muscles felt frozen.

'Charlie?'

Her eyes were unreadable. She spoke as slowly and as expressionlessly as an electronic robot.

'You knew about the grants?'

Now he had that dropping-down-a-lift-shaft feeling in his stomach. He shifted uneasily on his seat.

'Yes, but . . . '

He couldn't think of a way to continue. Her lashes lay on her cheeks briefly for a moment and then opened to reveal such shattering pain in her eyes that James wanted to cry out loud.

'You told me what you did,' she said softly, as if she were talking to herself. 'You told me that you bought property without caring what it was or who built it. You told me that all you cared about was selling it on and making a profit. How could I have forgotten?'

She lifted her head and James saw her throat quiver.

'God help me! You even warned me that you'd break up a place if there was more profit in it.'

James opened his mouth to tell her about business, how the real world worked in such matters, but his mouth was dry and his tongue was sticking to his lips. Charlie, his heart cried, Charlie, it's all going wrong. Her gaze met his with that brutal, unflinching honesty of hers.

'I'm making no mistake here,' she said in a tight voice. 'I'm not misjudging you. Your plan is to claim the grants, turn Deepdale into a wasteland and make a huge profit when you sell it, right?'

'Well, I wasn't sure if I was going to do it myself or just sell it to someone who knew how to maximise the opportunity,' James stammered.

He wished fervently that he had one of those glossy government brochures in his hand, that he could show

Charlie the way of the future — a single crop, efficient chemicals and machines. If only she'd stop looking at him like that.

He'd feel better if she raged at him, yelled or threw things. Instead there was only the icy silence and the feeling that he was adrift on an iceberg, an iceberg that was drifting every minute farther and farther away from land, warmth and safety and all the good things that made life worth living.

'Charlie?' he questioned, suddenly afraid.

Her stony gaze met his own. Her tone was lifeless.

'I'm very sorry that I couldn't give you more notice,' she said, 'but you can take it out of my wages in lieu.'

'What do you mean?'

'I mean that I quit,' she said, and there was no arguing. 'I mean that you had better start looking for a new farm manager, one who will help you, because I would take a gun and kill myself before I would lift a finger in your direction.'

And she walked out of the kitchen leaving James shaking and wondering how his proposal had gone so wrong.

9

Charlie was too busy to be miserable. She had wandered in a daze after leaving James in the kitchen, too stunned and dismayed by her discovery to get her mind into gear, too sickened to even notice the bright weather. She would have to make plans, pack, find somewhere to live. She knew that, but right now her pain and distress were so great, the shock so disabling, that all she could do was wander.

Like a lost soul she wandered over her land, the land that had been hers and would now be lost to her for ever. She was saying goodbye, she supposed, touching the stone walls for the last time, gazing her fill on the moors. Her heart was quivering inside her breast as she wandered, instinctively heading for the high hills, as if she could find comfort there.

Not far from the shepherd's cottage where she and James had sheltered from the storm, she came across a bay-coloured moorland pony. Its hunched, uneasy posture caught her attention. Even in the midst of her distress, she was too much the farmer to pass it by without checking that all was well. And when she came close, she saw that the mare was in labour, and was suffering. She rolled up her sleeves and approached, speaking softly to the terrified animal.

It was several more hours before the foal was finally born. The mare, her coat nearly black with the hot, foamy sweat from her labour, scrambled to her feet and gave a maternal whinny that came deep from inside her. The foal struggled to take control of its long, gangling legs and heaved itself up. It headed straight for the mother and began nursing.

Charlie watched them with fresh pain. She would never have children! She knew that she would never love another man, and so she would never have children. She let the foal have a short drink, and then she took the mare by the wiry black hairs of her mane and led her towards the shepherd's cottage. The foal followed on uncertain legs.

The cottage was just as they'd left it, but the straw den in front of the fire looked scruffy and forlorn. Charlie turned her back on it and busied herself with getting the mare comfortable. The foal began nursing again as the mare stuck her grateful nose in a bucket of cold water.

Charlie plaited a handful of straw together and began brushing the mare's coat. She might catch cold if the sweat weren't dried from her coat. As she brushed, Charlie marvelled at how quickly the mare seemed to have recovered from her ordeal. The delivery had been difficult and yet now the mare was drinking happily, her warm brown eyes turned on her offspring as if it had been all worthwhile. Nature was strong, Charlie thought, and the best rewards follow the most painful ordeals.

As she worked, she began to consider her position in a new light. She had not struggled against James and his scheme to ruin Deepdale. She had quit, run away in effect, leaving the way clear for him to do as he wished.

But I love him, her heart cried. How can I fight him? I'm not fighting the man, Charlie thought. I love the man with all my heart. What I'm fighting is his urge to destroy, to flatten all that is warm and worthwhile, in the name of profit. Why shouldn't I oppose that? There are other people who think the same way. I could look for support. I could organise a petition.

The mare was dry now. There was nothing for her to eat in the cottage, so Charlie led the pony out so that she could nibble on the sweet grass. The early-summer sunshine dazzled her after the darkness inside. She stood blinking, feeling as if she'd emerged from a prison, or a tomb.

She heard a well-known, shrill yap. It

was Bingo. The little white dog came rushing over to jump around her, frisking at her legs as if he was very pleased with himself. She shaded her eyes against the hot sun. A familiar figure was striding towards her. She could feel her heart pounding, and deep in her mind was the pain of knowing that they could never be together. But she stood calmly, waiting for him. The time for running was over.

James took the last few steps at a run. She saw with a shock that his eyes were soft and concerned.

'Charlie? Are you all right? What's happened to you?'

For the first time, she realised that she was not only soaked with the mare's sweat and her own, but liberally splattered with blood from the birthing process.

'It's all right,' she reassured him quickly, gesturing at the now-grazing mare. 'That's a new foal, and I helped.'

James barely gave the enchanting, long-legged foal a glance. His hands flew out as if he would grab her. Charlie didn't know if he wanted to shake her or wrap her up in his arms. It didn't matter. She wouldn't allow either. His eyes were fixed on her intently, yet she couldn't read the expression. That didn't matter either.

'I don't want you to go,' he said abruptly.

She lifted her chin.

'I'm not going,' she said, and she could hear the certainty in her voice that she was doing the right thing. 'I'm going to stay here and fight you, every way I know how. Maybe you'll win, maybe you won't, but I can't leave the place I was born in to the mercy of a destroyer.'

James made a movement towards her.

'I've been hunting for you for hours. I've got to tell you — '

She held up her hand to stop him.

'No! I've got to tell you! You told me agri-business is the way of the future. But it's only one way, James. Did you know that there are also government grants for farming ecologically? I could get a grant to plant hedgerows, for example, but I haven't applied for it because Deepdale is right with stone walls. Money isn't everything, James.'

She looked at him sadly.

'A government grant is not the right motive for changing something beautiful, something that works well as it is.'

'You are beautiful,' he said in reply, and she couldn't doubt his sincerity.

She had to protect herself from the love that she saw in his eyes. She wouldn't allow herself to be softened, to be talked into a wrong course of action just because she couldn't resist him.

'I'm going now,' she said abruptly. 'I'll get off your land.'

This time James did catch her arm. His touch was warm and electric. It started her trembling, but she drew back, fighting the magnetic pull she was feeling.

'I'm horrible,' she warned him. 'I'm covered with mucky stuff.'

'I don't care,' James said, pulling her to him.

She couldn't stop her eyes locking on his, but she could keep her body stiff. His nearness was torture, but she knew what she had to do, what she must say.

'But I do care,' she whispered.

Her arms were rigid at her side. She clenched her fists to still the longing she had to hold him, to just throw herself at him and forget all her principles.

'I do care,' she said again, and her voice was stronger. 'I care for what's right and what's natural. I care for Deepdale and everyone on it. I care for the right way of doing things. And, James, I'm going to fight for them.'

She had expected him to pull away, to walk off disgusted, but he held her and continued to look down on her and the emotion in his eyes was unnerving, full of warmth, love, laughter.

'James,' she said, more uncertainly, 'we'll be enemies.'

'No,' he said confidently.

'Yes,' she said sadly.

The warmth of his body seemed to reach out and tempt her. She could see a pulse beating at the open neck of his shirt. He was wearing his country clothing, she noted absently.

'Why aren't you wearing a suit?' she asked him suddenly. 'I thought you'd be changing, going back to London now you've got what you wanted.'

'I'm not going back to London. At least, I'll never live there again.'

His eyes were glowing with his feelings. Charlie looked up at him, astonished. What was he so happy about?

'Not going back?' she echoed.

'No,' he said. 'Oh, Charlie, it's my turn now to tell you a few things.'

She could see dark shadows under his eyes. He's had no sleep since the cave rescue, she thought, suppressing the urge to tell him to rest. Not that she'd had any sleep. Fatigue was doing strange things to her. She had a strange, floating sensation, as if the sunlit landscape around her wasn't real, as if it were just a painted backdrop for one man and one woman — a man who was smiling at her with so much love in his eyes that she felt dizzy.

'You have every right to look surprised,' he observed, 'but this isn't a quick decision, not really. It's been forming slowly in my mind.'

He shook his head and looked rueful.

'Although, initially, I'll admit, I was thinking in terms of buying a cottage with the profit from Deepdale.'

Charlie twisted in his arms, but she didn't pull away.

'Initially?' she queried.

She could feel her whole being, not daring to hope, exactly, but growing very still as she concentrated on his words.

'Let's sit down,' James suggested. 'I've got a lot to tell you.'

He pulled her down next to him on the sun-warmed turf. The smell of fresh grass rose around them. Bingo sat next to them, then put his nose on his paws and went to sleep. This time, when

James put his arms around her, Charlie found herself leaning into the strength of his muscled body. She twisted her head to look up at him. Had he understood how serious she was about fighting him?

James answered the question in her eyes, touching a light finger gently to her lips.

'I know what you want to say to me, Charlie, and I understand why. But let me try to explain to you why I behaved as I did.'

His voice trailed off. A shadow touched the blue of his eyes.

'I had a strange upbringing. You know my parents were divorced. They were too busy to bother with a small boy. They made sure I had plenty of money, of course. I used to think that I had everything, large allowance, good school, lots of freedom. A lot of boys envied me. I'm beginning to realise that I had nothing, however. No home, no family, no love, but I didn't know that, until I came here.'

He looked down at Charlie, and she saw that the shadow was leaving his eyes, rolling away like a cloud after a storm. The first tiny thread of happiness began to wind itself around her heart. Her lips parted, but James pressed them closed with that gentle finger once more. He resumed his story.

'Until I came here, and saw a different way of life, business was all I knew, all I cared about.'

He paused again, and this time Charlie was content to wait. Her eyes followed his, looking out over the green moorland and the rolling stone walls. She could hear the steady, contented munching of the moorland pony nearby. Larks sang in the blue sky. Charlie loved this landscape with all her heart, just as she loved the man who now held her close.

'It took me hours to find you,' he said, hugging her as he relived his loss. 'Perhaps it was for the best. I had plenty of time to think about losing you, about losing what I'd just found.'

'What had you found?' Charlie asked softly, pressing into his warm chest more closely.

Happiness flared in his voice as he answered.

'Life! Love! A challenge!'

He pushed Charlie so that she lay flat on her back in the warm green-smelling grass and propped himself up on his elbows, looking down at her face. She looked up at him and she could feel her lips smiling. She could feel her heart singing. Her sixth sense knew that happiness lay ahead, but her practical nature demanded he prove it.

'The challenge of fighting me?' she enquired, but she was confident enough to kiss the end of his nose as she said it.

James shook his head.

'The challenge of making an old-fashioned farm like Deepdale pay its way in today's modern world.'

Charlie felt excitement course through her veins.

'Do you think you could?'

'It'll mean a lot of work,' James said, but he looked as if he were facing the prospect with relish. 'I know more about smashing things up than making them pay. Running Deepdale is going to be the challenge of my life! But I could do it, I bet I could do it.'

James held out a hand and began ticking off ideas on his fingers.

'That second barn of yours, all you do is keep sacks in it. It would convert into three or four excellent holiday cottages. We could expand the bed and breakfast, maybe advertise in the caving magazines.'

'No farming?' Charlie asked, feeling a slight disappointment.

James nodded firmly.

'Yes, but we have to diversify. There's no way we can compete with agribusiness, so we have to be different. Maybe try some rare sheep and make cheese. Sam told me the tomatoes didn't pay, so why don't we grow garlic and ginger in those empty glass houses?'

We, Charlie thought blissfully. Her arms came up and went around him. He kissed her forehead. He met her eyes with an odd look of shyness.

'But I can only succeed if the woman I love is by my side,' he said softly. 'Oh, Charlie, I've been such a fool. I've loved you from the first moment I saw you, but I was fighting it. How could I admit that everything I'd believed before was wrong! That's a big pill for any man to swallow.'

His tone was regretful.

'Even this morning, only a few hours ago, I came close to throwing away everything I want most in the world. Can you forgive me?'

'There's nothing to forgive,' Charlie said softly.

He still looked shy, hesitant.

'I hardly dare ask you, but will you, could you, do you think you could marry me?'

Charlie felt as if all the sunshine of summer was warming her heart as she met the shy and tender love in his eyes.

She couldn't speak. James gathered her up close and held her, still anxious.

'I've changed,' he promised her, and she could read the sincerity in his eyes. 'Don't worry that I'll want to go back to the city. What I had before was a pale imitation. This is real. My love for you is real.'

His anxiety deepened. His eyes pleaded as he looked down at her.

'Oh, Charlie, say you'll marry me, do.'

Charlie found her voice at last.

'I will,' she breathed softly.

She felt James's relief running through his whole body. He threw his head back and laughed at the sky.

'She'll marry me!' he crowed, and then he looked back at her, his eyes intent and serious, happy and loving. 'Oh, Charlie!' he said, and she couldn't help smiling back at the laughter in his voice, the love in his eyes. 'When I set out to buy a farm, I never imagined this kind of profit!'

'Think of it as a harvest instead.'

His loving eyes met hers.

'The rich harvest of your love!'

'Of our lives together,' Charlie said, smiling.

THE END